D0649786

FLIPSIDE FICTION
Because There Are Always Two Sides to Every Story

Alex The Great

Alex

by
Barbara S. Cole

T 39148

THE ROSEN PUBLISHING GROUP, Inc.
NEW YORK

Published in 1989 by The Rosen Publishing Group, Inc.
29 East 21st Street, New York, NY 10010

First Edition

Manufactured in the United States of America

Library of Congress Cataloging-In-Publication Data

Cole, Barbara S.
    Alex the great./by Barbara S. Cole.—1st ed.
        p.   cm. —(Flipside fiction)
    Issued back-to-back/head to toe.
    Summary: Presents two viewpoints about teens and drugs, one from a girl on drugs and one from a friend who tries to help her.
    [1. Drug abuse—Fiction.]   I. Title.   II. Series.
PZ7.C673414A1   1988   [Fic]—dc19   88-37104
ISBN 0-8239-0941-7

Manufactured in the United States of America

ALEX THE GREAT
ALEX
Chapter One

It's like this: I think clothes are what make you what you are. Do birds have color? Sure. And birds are just birds when you pluck out their feathers. Not a pretty sight. One might be a little bigger or a little smaller, but under those pretty feathers it's just drumsticks, a beak, and a pair of grimy claws. Anyone who wants to be anybody is the same way. Strip the threads off a rock star and you've got one puny little bag of bones jumpin' around on stage like a skeleton of Pinocchio. Like, what's a peacock without feathers? Just a naked turkey. What's the difference between a Japanese sumo wrestler and The Incredible Hulk? You got it. Their duds. Well, maybe a little green dusting powder, too. When I think about it, when I go back in my head as far back as I can, clothes are what got me into all this in the first place.

I'm not the world's greatest writer, but somewhere in this thing I'll be able to put down what I mean. Since I woke up from the dead, things have been clear as mud, I swear.

When I first woke up, I was cold because the wind was blowing in through an open window to the left of my bed. I think I had been dreaming that my friend Deonna was standing next to me and I was cryin' or something goofy like that. Maybe those nurses thought I'd never wake up so they were trying to make more bed space by chilling me out. There's no law that says you can't pull the plug on a patient by blasting her with cold air, ya know. I remember thinking, wow, if this is heaven, it looks like a hospital room with a beast hanging from the ceiling. That turned out to be Dr. Edwards staring right into my face, leaning over the rails of my bed. Maybe I thought he was Deonna in my dream, I don't know. First thing he says to me out of his hairy black beard is, "Ummm. Pupils slightly dilated, but normal." Then he leaves this yellow notebook on the table next to my bed. He had two more just like it under his arm along with a metal clipboard. I wonder if he does his rounds dropping off notebooks at the beds of all the crazies like they probably do in the Army when they hand out the uniforms at boot camp? Regulation pants, regulation belt. Regulation banana slug notebook.

I wanted to reach for it to see if he had written anything in it, but I was afraid to move my arm because there was this tube stuck into my vein right at the wrist. I never shot. Needles give me the willies. Even when I wanted to kill myself, and I knew that one pop in the ropes would do the trick neater than anything else, I didn't go for it. You could get AIDS that way! I thought, what if I botched the job and someone found me too soon? Then I'd croak really gnarly and slow from pneumonia or from brain damage. So needles have always been on the outs with me.

Then I think I watched TV when this nurse with really bad eye makeup came in and handed me a channel changer. She said she'd take the tube out of my arm the next morning. I think for a minute she just stared at me. It was eerie the way she looked. Kind of like a clown and a ghost. She should get together with Edwards. Their kid would look like a cross between a see-through bean sprout, a clown, and a gorilla.

The kid would probably grow up to be, you know, the kinda guy who never got sick and had lots of babies. Then there'd be little shrinks everywhere. . . like ants. Ugh. Couldn't you see it? The kid's first word would be "Ummm."

Anyway, the Beast turns out to be a shrink, and he tells me that it's gonna be a while before I can put all the pieces together. Well, I faked it like I knew exactly where I was and told him I liked my privacy, thank you very much. Before he left, he told me that it might help to try and write things down. He said that, if I started a new thought on a separate page, when the missing pieces came to me I could just fill everything in until I got a clear picture. But hey, I'm not into reading or writing, so what does this dude think he's pulling? Maybe I'll snap up a magazine once in a while, but just to get an eyeful of the clothing. I'm no goober, but you know, I'd rather spend my time on something else. Whatever it was that I liked to do besides coke marathons and daydreamin' about clothes, I can't remember right now. But maybe it'll all come back to me.

Sometimes its kinda hard to figure out exactly what happened first, or when everything started, for that matter. When I want to think, I can't think straight, and when I want to stop thinking, I can't. Can you believe it? They didn't even give me anything to make me sleep in the hospital. I remember that for two whole nights while I was in there, I lay awake staring out the window. That's what made me think about birds when I started this thing out. Those feathered rats wouldn't shut up, even at night. Somebody ought to do something about that.

So here I sit, broken-hearted. No, just kidding. That's what everybody writes in the bathroom stalls at school like it's the first poem they ever heard. I'm still here, but I have another room now on the other side of the hospital. It's where they put the nuts. I should've known I'd wind up like this. It's just like Deonna used to say. She'd say, "Alex, you're crazy. You keep doing the works the way you are, and you'll wind up dead." And I'd tell her that doctors have been using coke for eons and eons. And now what's wrong with my brain? Nothin'. Okay, okay, so maybe it's true. I did swallow just about everything left over from my stash and blew my brains straight to the stars. And here I am, in the nut house with a couple of pimple-faced goobers who really have it bad. I feel so sorry for them. Ha ha.

For starters, there's Larry. This guy's perfect for this place. Larry has the stringiest, dirtiest hair I have ever seen on anyone, and that includes my friend Rabbit, who hardly ever took a shower. Even though everything is kept so clean here that sometimes you wish you had a big bowl of mud to throw at the wall just to get a change of scenery, Larry always seems to be dirty. It's because he's afraid to wash up at the sink. See, when he washes his face, that means he has to close his eyes. He's afraid someone's gonna get him from behind when he leans over the sink with soap in his eyes. And he cries all the time, for any reason you can think of. I've seen him sit there in our therapy group, serious as one of those Mozart statues that people put on their pianos, and then like a fade-in slide show just change his face completely. He should have gone into the movies. In two minutes, I swear the guy can go from serious listening to crying so bad that we all think he's going to choke to death, and then he goes all the way to laughing like one of those little plastic gizmos you can buy where you hit a button and a voice laughs for five minutes so hard that you want to smash it to shut it up. But that's not how it works in our group meetings. You have to sit there and wait until this guy "works through his emotions." If you ask this nerdy crybaby why he's bawling his eyes out, he'll shrug his shoulders like he doesn't know. His nose will run and his eyes will get all bloodshot and he's just like a walkin' skeleton because he won't eat the food here. He's afraid someone's gonna get him. He doesn't know why.

The counselors, Sam and Janine, really get after him when he goes off into space, crying and blowing his nose and talking about how sometime he's gotta eat and would they please let him into the kitchen before dinner so he can see if tonight's his night to die. He has this thing about being prepared for death. Maybe he figures it's okay to croak as long as you have twenty-four hours' notice. I don't know what he's gonna do if somebody tells him it's his turn, but the guy's desperate to know. They ask him, "Who's going to poison you, Larry? Why do you think someone wants to do that to you, Larry?" And he curls up and cries some more and never answers them. This kinda thing goes on every single day, sometimes three times a day, which is how many times we all have to get together and tolerate each other.

I sit in there and think about how I got a real bad break, how I'm gonna just let this whole thing go by without really getting into it, and when I'm outta here, how I'm gonna do something amazing like graduate and go to design school. Then, just when I've got this totally decent plan going on in my head, when I can picture it like it's kind of a real cartoon, only with me as the star, one of the counselors will say it's my turn to "deal with my feelings" and then I have to come up with something. It's amazing how you can just split yourself into two people; one of me is listening to them and talking about "woe-is-me" because I know they like that kind of stuff, and the other me, the real one, is planning on how to get the heck outta this firetrap they call a hospital.

I mean, how bad could it be? I call up Deonna, and ask her to get me some clothes and try to scrape up some money. Then I change my name to something designer-like, you know, with a lot of accent marks over it, somethin' like Désirée, and hot-foot it to another city. Somewhere where I can get an easy job like waitressing in a sleaze-bag diner. Nobody would know who I was and I'd get a fresh start. I could rent a room after a little while, and it wouldn't be long before I could get hold of a sewing machine. Okay, so I don't know how to work a sewing machine. But how hard could it be? You just push the fabric through. Or maybe I'd get famous for my hand-sewn clothes. Nobody would know that I couldn't even sew a hem. The stuff I made would be so outrageous that they'd think the sloppy seams were part of the whole idea. You can't keep someone like me back, man. I don't belong in this crazy-house. I don't need to deal with my feelings. My feelings tell me to get outta here! And how good is it to sit there for hours and watch a guy who got a bad batch of rock freak over whether his tapioca pudding is gonna do him in? It's just bad luck. That's all it is for me, too. 'Cept I've still got all my brain cells and that grease-ball Larry doesn't. He's never gonna improve and he'll have to be sent to a permanent funny farm.

But me, I'm gonna escape. And only Deonna will know where to find me. If she helps me out just once more, I'll send her a check for $50,000 once I get famous. I'll even let her run my company. Well, that's if I can convince her that my clothes aren't what she calls "trash." Deonna thinks that anything that isn't tennis togs or warm-ups is loud and raggy. I'll call my first line Alex the Great so everybody at Edison High will know where the stuff came from. And I'll be famous. Like I said, how hard could it be? At least it wouldn't be as hard as what Deonna has to do to get famous. It wouldn't be as sweaty, that's for sure.

Not everybody in the program is like Larry. And not everybody has to stay in the hospital, either. It's the six of us for the most part, if you include the counselors and Dr. Edwards, and I bet none of us really expects anything to change. It's all some big stinkin' joke. It's gotta be.

I mean, how can you change from being a ditz-brain like Larry to a normal person after wiping out half your brain cells on crack? It's his own fault, too. He shoulda bought his junk from me and this wouldn't have happened. But you just can't tell some people some things.

What do these white coats expect to do with punks who are all splatted out and good for nothing, anyway? And how do you get like Lisa, who can't use the left half of her body and can't speak very well but is so mad all the time that she screams and throws fits because she can't do what she wants to anymore? Talk about tragedy, man. Lisa has everything you'd ever want to have. The cutest face, these really perfect, white, straight teeth, and blue eyes that just scream out of her head when she looks at you. But most of the time, she's not looking at anything. Her eyes roll up in her head sometimes when she has fits. You practically expect her head to twist around and around and around like she's that possessed girl in *The Exorcist*. It's no treat to see, let me tell you. Top all that off with a body that you can usually only see on a store mannequin and long, incredibly black hair that is almost blue, even under these fluorescents. If she went to my school, she'd probably be the head song leader or something. She'd have whatever guy she wanted, for sure. But not anymore. It's all over for her. I don't think she even knows this, but she drools sometimes. I mean, you'll be sitting there on the couch next to her and this long string of connected spit will just start running down into her lap. She doesn't try to wipe it off her face or get a tissue and clean herself up. Her mouth hangs open and she just kinda stares and drools and nothin' can snap her out of it. And then all of a sudden she does come out of it for no good reason at all. I can't figure it out.

We're going to have a parents' day this week when The Fluff and Larry's and Lisa's folks all come in for most of the day. I bet Lisa's folks are the kind that think once she gets out of this program she'll be okay. They probably know that she's not whacko all the time, and think that this means they can hope she gets normal again. But I know better. I've seen people just flip out and never come back. Dudes who shove all kinds of junk up their noses for years are fine. Then one day they get a bad batch or their mood is weird and doesn't mix too good with whatever they're doin' and next thing ya know they're dumb as a baby before it gets zapped with personality.

Dave always told me not to worry about that kind of thing happening to me. And when a guy like that tells you something, you listen! So I never worried because I knew he was giving me only the best stuff to sell. Real quality, hardly cut, smooth as silk and all that. When I first started to deal his stuff at school, I felt funny, like maybe someone would croak and it would all be on my head. That kind of guilt is enough to make you kill yourself, I mean it.

"Doesn't it bother you sometimes," I asked him after the first time we got together on a deal, "that maybe you'll give somebody a bad batch and they'll wig out on it? I mean, wouldn't you kinda feel funny about it?"

"Nah. You've got to realize that there's all different kinds of dealers, just like there's all different kinds of people in the world. Some don't care what they sell off, just as long as they make a buck. But me, I like to handle only the best. Some of us have class. Like you, for instance. And like me. See, I test it myself. If I like it, I know you'll like it. Some people are just coke pigs and rock hounds. There's no hope for people like that. They don't care what happens to them anyway. You're doing society a favor, Alex. These people will find something else and do it to death, like boozing or bike racing. But you, you're a quality dealer now, make no mistake about it. And you'll know when to stop, too. You'll make a buck or two and lay it down for something even better. Just like me. I'm not going to wear a suit and do the old nine to five every day. And I'm not going to be a cop, like my dad. This is just a means to an end. I'm going to buy real estate and stocks and live on the interest."

"What if you get caught first? Aren't you kinda afraid of that?"

"Who's going to narc on me? Look at the whole picture, Alex. I'm a top-seeded varsity tennis player. That means I get great grades in school because nobody has the guts to give me a bad grade and keep me off the team when we're creaming everyone in the district. I wear white all the time, like a good little angel. I keep myself tan and in shape, and my hair is cut shorter than my dad's when he was in high school. Then, if you really want to feel safe, take a look at my dad. He's been on the force forever, and almost all the guys who work with him got into it because he made it easy for them to join up. They all owe him something, and guys stick together that way. Nobody would say a word. So he gets this really easy neighborhood beat where everybody can see what a nice guy he is, and who would think that a guy like that would have a son like me who did anything illegal? Besides, there are worse things, like bank robbery and murder. This is real white-collar kind of stuff, and if they catch one guy they blow it all out of proportion to try to make you feel paranoid."

"Guess you've got it all wired, huh," I said, feeling a little better about not getting caught, at least.

"Yeah, and nothing can go wrong, mark my words. This way, everybody's happy, and nobody gets hurt. It's a win-win kind of situation. A sure thing."

Chapter Two

Just once, I wish they'd take each one of us off somewhere and explain what this is all about. First thing this morning, we played this game called Hot Seat. It's where you have to take turns asking all kinds of questions that you normally couldn't get away with. The kinda questions that your mom tells you are rude or nosy to ask. It was so crazy that I wanted to get outta there. And when Deonna comes to visit today, I'm layin' it out completely for her. She's gotta help me bust this bistro, man. It's like I'm desperate for freedom, especially after this morning's little game.

After they laid out the rules, Sam and Janine moved to the far corner of the room they had us in. It's called the Workroom. We're supposed to be getting better in there. But wow, whatta scam. I think someone should look into this program pretty carefully. These guys are totally whacked out! So they sat back and let us play this Hot Seat game. Larry got to ask one question from either Lisa or me, and then whoever he asked had to answer without lying, even once. Then that person got to ask me a question, and so on like that. First I thought, God, this is going to put me back to sleep for sure. But then Larry asked Lisa how she felt about having her perfect face go lopsided, and Lisa freaked.

"It's not! Nothing's wrong with me or my face. It's your

face that's ugly, Larry. Let's talk about the red volcanoes on your face. Or the craters or the blackheads or the black hair you've got all over your chin because they don't trust you with a razor in the bathroom? Huh? Huh?"

Larry reminded me of those guys in school that Deonna used to call "bugs." What Lisa said was true. If you shrunk Larry down enough, he'd sort of look like a spider.

"Lisa, before you can ask a question, you've got to answer Larry's first," Janine said. Larry looked like he was going to start crying, which was nothin' new.

Then Lisa started twitching and saying, "Okay. Okay. Okay. But I don't know. I'm fine. Okay. Okay."

Larry looked back at the counselors with this big smirk on his face. "How are we going to play Hot Seat if one of us won't quit spazzing out?"

"Just give her a little extra time. Some people take longer to answer than others, Larry," Sam said. Sam is a pretty big guy who acts like he's on 'ludes all the time. Nothin' fazes him, I swear. I think I like him the best of anybody in this place because you can tell just by lookin' at him that he really cares about what he's doing, even if it never does any good.

So we sat there waiting for Lisa to come around for about ten minutes and it seemed like forever, but finally, when she didn't stop stuttering, Janine asked Larry to send me a question. He got this really evil look in his eye and grinned a little bit while he thought up something to ask me. And I thought, hey, why me? How come he gets to ask another question? This isn't how the rules are supposed to go! But my idea was to just put one over on these idiots and wait until Deonna came later on. Just get through it one more time, I told myself, 'cause you won't have to play these stupid games much longer. So I kept my trap shut.

"Okay, I've got a good one now," Larry said. "How many times a day do you still feel like you have to cop a buzz?" Then he sat back and stared at me with a look on his pimply face like he got me back for something I never did to him in the first place.

"Whadda ya mean, STILL wanna get high," I said, "I don't ever HAVE to, ya know. You act like I'm a real doper. No way!"

"Alex, this game isn't therapeutic if you don't tell the absolute truth," Janine said.

"I AM TELLIN' THE TRUTH," I yelled, "and ya know what else? I hardly ever even think about it. And I never did before, either. You guys think I have some kinda problem, but that's your problem! There's nothing wrong with me at all. I'm just in here so I don't have to go to Wintersburg this fall, that's all, and that's the absolute truth."

"She's lying. She's not playing the game," Larry said to the counselors.

"We can't force someone to talk about something they aren't ready to deal with yet, Larry. Let's just get on with the game, shall we? Alex, it's your turn now." Janine looked over at Lisa and saw that she was still staring at nothing, so she pointed at me to ask Larry something.

Well, I can tell you, by that time I was pissed. This filthy little nothin' of a guy was tryin' to corner me into making it look like I'm just as bad a nut case as he is. And he's a schitzed-out paranoid cokehead goober with an awful lotta nerve, for sure. Well, I said to myself, what am I gonna do with this dirt bag? Then it came to me...the perfect revenge.

"Okay, Larry, as long as we're all tellin' the truth here, I guess I gotta level with you. I do kinda have a problem. It's like this: I'm not real good at keeping secrets. See, this morning, I heard the floor nurse talking to the nutritionist outside my door. They caught me listening in and told me to keep it under my hat, but like I said, that's part of my problem. I just can't help but leak it to ya. What I heard them say was that it was time to do somethin' pretty special with your dinner. Before I got caught, I even heard one of 'em say, "Yep. Tonight's the night." Now tell the truth, dude, what do ya think of that, really?"

Larry's pupils looked like a pair of those old 45 rpms. They got so big that I thought they'd spread out all over his eyeballs. He was spooked, for sure, and it set him off on a crying binge even more hairy than some of the ones I had already seen, when I thought he was going to die from being dehydrated from losing all those tears.

And that was the end of the game. Lisa never came around enough so that she could play. You could look at her and almost see the nerve endings in her brain explode in teeny weenie fireworks about a zillion times a second. The kid was a real mess, but nothin' compared to Larry, who turned into a blob of melted Jello, the way he blubbered and carried on about not wanting to eat ever again for the rest of his life.

Now maybe you could say that it was just a little bit mean of me to do that to him, since I knew that one of the leftovers from doing all that snow was that he was a maxed-out paranoid on a deep bummer. You don't need to be a doctor to see it, either. But hey, the guy was out to get me and I had to stop him. It's like nothin's fair, ya know? I mean, what nerve to make it out like I was a stoner. Like I didn't have any control over what I used to do, and worse, he just assumed that I was like him, always wanting more blow, no matter how bad it was. Well, I showed him, didn't I? Bet they'll have to stick an IV in his arm by tomorrow because they won't be able to cram any food down his warped little face. That scuzz-bomb!

It gets to be like some kind of joke when you sit there watching this stuff hour after hour. I mean, come on! Is this guy Larry planted here for some reason? Or because I even think that he is, does that make me paranoid, too? Sometimes you wanna just get up and slap one of the counselors and tell them to lay off the poor idiot. It's a lost cause. This guy's never gonna be able to get out of here and live a half-way normal kind of life. I, for one, won't go up to him at breaks and talk to him because anything I say could make him slobber all over me like he does with the others. I got my own problems. Lotsa problems. It was easier before. I thought I had it wired and then bingo bango, I wake up and my head's fulla birds screaming. I'm a prisoner here! Help!

Well, I'm not really a prisoner. I did have a choice, if you can call it that. The Fluff and Dr. Edwards got together and then, before they gave me a choice of what was going to happen to me, my mom and I had a little talk. She looked different that day. I was laid out in that bed, and since I couldn't sleep very well I was wired and tired at the same time. I couldn't keep my attention on her for very long, and I think Edwards clued her in or something, because she said, "I'll keep this short. I haven't been able to work steadily because I've been worried sick about you, so the airline is on my back to get me to straighten up about my hours. But I don't know if I should stay on with them because that depends on what happens with you. I guess I didn't know what was happening to you because I wasn't around enough. Anyway, I want you to get better, and Dr. Edwards says if we put you into this rehabilitation program, you stand a good chance of doing all right. So that's my vote. After that, we'll just have to see how it goes."

"What's the other choice?" I asked. She never spoke to me that way before. She looked like an old lady sittin' there. Before all this happened, she would never have worn a blouse with so much as a thread out of place. But she had on a grubby work shirt and not a stitch of makeup on her face. Her voice was low and sounded kinda like she had a lid on it. Sort of hollow like she was holding a lot back. Maybe she always talked like that, but I don't remember it. She was frazzed. Even her hair looked frazzed. It was pulled back into a ponytail, but since it's so straight, most of it was hanging down the sides of her face. I wished she'd pull that one hair away from her eyelid. Every time she blinked, it would curve and bob and bother the heck out of me, like a mosquito buzzin' around your head in the dark. It was gettin' on my nerves to say the least. But I didn't reach over and move it for her. We never touched like that.

"You go to Wintersburg."

Wintersburg! I thought to myself, God, you gotta be kidding. I'd get creamed over there! The only people who go to The Burg are the kind who would eat you if you didn't give them your lunch, your clothes, and all your money whenever they asked for it. Kids over there are huge! I mean radically mean. You know how there's just some puppies in a litter that you can tell won't ever sit or heel or learn to poop outside? Well, these guys at The Burg are just like that. It's scary what they've pulled. They've all been to The Hall more than a few times for doing things like running a guys' legs over and over with their motorcycles and just grabbing someone and raping them on the side of a building. I heard somewhere that they stash you away at The Burg and let you play Ping Pong in the classes because they know that you won't amount to anything except a jailbird once you get out. And when you turn eighteen, they probably parole someone just to make extra room for you in the slammer. It's freaky how it's so planned out. No way was I going to Wintersburg, no way!

At Edison, there's all kinds of people jumbled up together, but mostly blacks and Chicanos. There's fights and everything, but nothing like you'd come up against at The Burg. Mostly, everybody just hangs out in their own groups and keeps to themselves. If I had to go back to school, then it would be Edison over Wintersburg any day, so that's how I got here, in the Drug Abuse Rehabilitation Program at General. Some choice, man.

That day when my mom came, I asked her about Deonna.

I knew that my mom probably didn't even remember who she was, because every time Deonna came over, my mom was either asleep or getting ready to leave for a few days. My mom didn't really know who my friends were, come to think of it. Not that I had tons of them. I mean, how many punks can you trust when you're carryin' around a thousand bucks worth of goodies in your book bag every day?

She said, "That was part of your past. You'd better forget about that black girl with all the muscles. It's time to make new friends. You don't realize what kind of trouble you're in."

So I was sittin' there looking at her with that orangy, scrawly hair of hers sticking to her pasty face, thinking, who are you to tell me who I can see and who I can't? What's it to ya? If you wanted to keep track of things, you should have been around more often, like Deonna's folks are. I mean, it's not like Deonna has it so easy being herself, either. Her mom is the real starchy type who thinks that only guys should be strong. Deonna once said that her mom wanted her to cut down on her practicing time and maybe prepare herself for somethin' more practical like nursing school. But when it comes right down to it, I think my friend has it easier than I do. She knows what her parents want her to do, but at least she still gets to be herself. Me, I can't seem to get close enough to my mom so that she even knows who I am!

The Fluff is kinda like Lisa, the spazz. She just goes through the program, from one meeting to the next, not really caring what they say to her or what she has to do. If they say, okay, it's art therapy time, Lisa draws. If they slap a rowing machine in front of her, she rows until they tell her to stop. The Fluff is like that. She thinks she has to tell me what to do now because when she wasn't around I messed up. She does it because she thinks that's what she's supposed to do. But whoa, let's get real here for a minute. I never asked to be born, ya know. Maybe it's true she had to work that slimy job to buy me food and clothes and pay the rent, but nobody said she had to take a leave of absence just so she could sit by my bed and cry the whole time when I bonked out for a little while. Hey, I was fine, I was just taking a long nap. Sometimes it's good to do that.

Where was she before, when it coulda been nice to have a mom around? Off in Hong Kong. And don't think it didn't make me feel really bad when I saw her putting vaseline on her teeth so her lips wouldn't get cracked from smiling all day and night at those businessmen. That kinda thing could make anybody feel humiliated. I just got sick of feelin' bad, that's all. It wasn't my fault she got pregnant with me. I had nothin' to do with it. It wasn't like there wasn't some kind of birth control back in the days when she was a teenager, ya know. And even if there wasn't, who said she had to go and fall in love with a sailor? Everybody knows how those guys are. I mean I can understand fallin' for a guy who looks so perfect in his uniform and who promises you everything, but let's face it, man, the ship that comes in also goes out, and she should have known better. So he ships out and she's stuck with me for the rest of her life. It's not like I don't understand it, but hey, a girl has to fend for herself in this world, right?

Chapter Three

Anyways, I'm sittin' here getting myself all worked up in this banana slug notebook just to kill time before Deonna comes, and I can't wait. My pal, Deonna. It's true that when the chips are down, nobody can save you but yourself, and nothin's better than having a real friend. One you can trust enough to tell anything to. Someone who will be on your side no matter how low things get. The one person who can dig me outta this pit they call a hospital is Deonna. She has never let me down, ever. It gives me lotsa hope just thinking about how things have always been between us.

Deonna's got this uncle, I think his name's Raymond or something, and he used to come over Deonna's house at the worst times after being out all night partyin'. I'm thinkin' about this now because I just thought about her uncle and how he went into a treatment program too. He was into boozin', which I don't think too much of, compared to other things. I guess everyone has their "jones" about somethin'. Some people go crazy over money, and some people cram food in their faces until they're big as blimps. I think people can even get crazed over love just like it's any other drug. That makes me wonder whatever happened to that guy, Raymond. I hope he's not locked up somewhere like this place!

Anyways, Deonna called me up one night when I was all by myself, enjoyin' some sounds and other stuff, as usual. She said her uncle was sicker than a dog, and it was true 'cause I could hear him ralphing it up in the bathroom even though Deonna said her bedroom door was closed. That's the kind of thing that grossed Deonna out, and she couldn't get to sleep. So I played a great dance tune to her over the phone and I even shared my party mood with her by dancin' in the living room so she could sort of join in, even though she couldn't leave her house. That's the kind of pal I've been to her. You know, the kind who gets concerned when her friend can't sleep and all that.

And I remember this other time, too, when I was walking home from school. It was after I had already seen Deonna on the courts but didn't really know who she was yet. And it was just before I started gettin' so popular because of the stuff I was selling.

Anyways, I was walking home from school like I said, and I was wearin' something jazzy that I had made up myself. I didn't care if nobody wore stuff like that. I just have a thing for glitter and sequins and shiny silver studs and stuff, that's all. Well, I guess the Chicano girls didn't think my taste was so fine, and just after I turned this corner near the school they surrounded me. I swear it was a sea of hairspray, man! There must have been about fifteen girls around me, poking me and pushing me into the middle of this circle they were making. I practically freaked! Then this kinda fat one came up to me, I mean right up into my face, and grabbed a hold of my blouse and pulled on it! I jerked away from her.

"Let go of my duds, Fats," I said.

She turned to the other ones around her and said, "Hey, Red here thinks I'm fat. Didja hear that?"

"Take her face off, man," someone yelled.

"Nobody talks to Zoila like that, Red," the fat one said to me. Then she shoved me backwards.

"The name's Alex, Fats," and I shoved her back. Well, by this time I knew I was in for a fight, even though I never had to fight before in junior high because I was always the biggest one there. We started shoving each other, and once I even tried to slip away and get through the crowd, but that only made this Zoila girl madder. She knocked me down on the ground and started pullin' my hair so hard that it made my eyes water. And then all of a sudden everything stopped and people moved away from us. This black girl yanked Zoila up by the strap on the back of her leather jacket and just dropped her back down to the side of me like she was made of feathers or something! Then she stood there looking at Zoila with her hands on her hips and this mean look on her face. Everybody was whispering "Whoa. Who's that?" When I got all the hair out of my face, I saw that it was Deonna. She helped me up and said, "Start walking before their guys show up." So I did. And me and her walked right out of that crowd. It was a miracle, I tell ya! Then about half a block away Deonna said that she better walk me part of the way home, just in case something else happened.

I mean it was like Superman comin' to save me, 'cept she was just this girl I had seen around school, not anybody special as far as I could tell. And, of course, she was really strong or there would be no way I could have survived that crowd by myself, that's for sure.

"Thanks," I said. "I don't know why you did it, but thanks a lot. I was gettin' creamed in there."

"It could have been a lot worse for you, you know. It's a good thing I didn't take the bus today, huh?"

"Guess I'm just lucky you're not like them. That Zoila girl was a fat mess," I said.

Deonna was shorter than me and not really pretty or anything, but she had a nice smile and, like I already said, she had muscles coming outta her ears! Then she asked me where I got my clothes. I told her I shopped in used clothing stores and put the outfits together myself. Sometimes I would glue on old-lady jewelry to kinda spruce everything up. She liked it and said so. I wasn't used to being around someone who just said what was on her mind like that.

I told her, "Someday maybe, if I can get up enough money, I'm gonna go to a design school and have my own line of clothes."

"Maybe you could get a scholarship," she said.

"Me? Huh, you gotta be kidding. I can't get into school at all. If I show up to class and try a little bit, I can pull a C, but that doesn't happen too often. I've gotta find some other way," I said.

"That's what I'm after. If I can get a scholarship, I'll have a chance at the big time," she said.

"What big time? In what?"

"Tennis. I don't work out for nothing, you know," she smiled.

"Well, even if it all falls apart, I'm glad you came around when you did. I think I'll be okay from here on. I don't live much farther anyway. Hey, thanks again. See ya around, okay?"

I remember how she looked right then. Just like I made her whole day when I said, "See ya around." And I did see her around all the time. Sometimes I used to pass the tennis courts just to sneak up and watch her practice. Wow. What an arm on that girl! It was exciting, that's all, because you just don't see someone play that hard, like their whole life depended on it!

People thought I was wigged out, I just knew it by the way they looked at me, but after that fight they looked at Deonna the same way. Well, so what if they thought me and her were freaks of nature, man! Who cared, when we could hang out together like we were somethin' special! I didn't know Deonna hardly at all back then, but I knew I liked her because there wasn't a mean bone in her body. And she was like me. Different. I mean, not because she's black, but because she was so hyped about bein' a tennis star someday. She'd work out with weights and then go running, and then play a few hours of tennis, then go home and get all her homework done. And without even cheatin', either! I knew that was pretty amazin', because it wasn't anything I could do myself.

Normally, I guess she and I would have nothin' to do with each other. But nobody hung out with her because they just couldn't figure her out. What girl has muscles like she does? I know those bumps don't come naturally to girls, so it meant she had to put in a lot of hours to get 'em. And it didn't look bad, either, but it sure kept her off to herself most of the time. So I thought, me and her, we're kinda alike, even though we're not.

So my best friend in the whole universe for the past two years has been Deonna Johnson. She was really decent to me from the start. And later on, it was great to have her around. I mean, when I graduated into heavy dealin' and all that. It blew the competition away to see us. I had all the goods, and if they got in my way Deonna would lay them flat and they all knew it. I made a lot of money thanks to her. I can't wait to see her today, either. Because today we're talkin' freedom! Aya!

So except for once so far, I'm here until Dr. Edwards lets me out. And then once I'm out I have to keep comin' back like I'm on a mental patient parole. They want to make sure I don't snort, or stay out past curfew, or hang around anyone who is "bad" for me. And they want to make sure that I don't try to kill myself again.

Last week, I got to go home for a few hours. It was weird. Sam told me that I had to remember everything I did and everything I thought about and write it down. Then come back at the end of the day and read to everyone in the group what I wrote. So The Fluff came to get me. She had a banged-up yellow Falcon. Were things that bad that she had to drive a car over twenty years old? The inside smelled like someone had been living in it, and there were big rusted holes in the floor so you could see through to the street as it whizzed underneath the car. That's what I did on the way to our apartment, just looked through the holes at the street, because there was nothin' to say to my mom. I couldn't believe they were lettin' me out. I hadn't been home in about three weeks. That morning when Dr. Edwards came by for his visit and said I was going home for the day, first I thought, great! Now I can skip out completely. I thought the first thing I'd do was call Deonna and we'd think of some way that I could just clear out. Like she could send me my clothes. But I'd have to get her a key to the place, and if Mom wasn't working anymore, she wouldn't know when to come in and box things up for me. But I didn't know anything. Man, was I out of it then! At first, I figured that if I ran off, for one, I'd have nowhere to go. And then there was this little voice in the back of my head that kept tellin' me I was gonna wind up like a street person, the kind you see downtown that have little paper signs saying "Homeless. Out of work. Hungry. Thank you and God bless you." I saw myself covered with little crawly bugs from not taking showers and my hair matted so it looked like a giant red hornet's nest. My teeth would be knocked out, and my clothes would stink like one of those portable bathrooms. It would be like that because there'd be no hope. I couldn't get a job doin' anything but box-girl or cleaning work, and if that was the case I'd just kill myself for sure. But now it's all planned out in my head, just like a great movie script. It's not gonna happen like that. I'll never be a bum. Somehow I'm gonna make it.

See, deep down I know I'm not that kind of a person. I was meant to be somebody special. It's just that things haven't been set up my way exactly. I mean, if I had it my way I would have a father who got upset at me if I didn't get good grades. One of those model types with slicked down hair and horned-rimmed glasses who help you with your math and expect you to be another Einstein. The kind of father that wears a giant college ring and works extra long hours so you can get a car when you're sixteen and go to the college he went to. He would want you to have a decent job so that someday, when he wasn't around to protect you, you could take good care of yourself. And then, if it was my way, I would have my mom join all these clubs and get to know lots of neat people who could help me out. She would be the type who donates money to charity and registers people to vote before elections. Her mail would always have those big square envelopes jammed full of invitations, like I've seen at some of the other kids' houses. Then, if I wanted to be what I've always dreamed of being, you know, a clothes designer, my dream mom would know all the right people to get things off the ground. But that's not how it is, and that's just tough.

Chapter Four

The first thing I did when we got home was walk over to the stereo to flip on some tunes. I was pretty hyped to be home because I never expected to see that dinky place again, and music always calmed me down somehow. The amp was lit up when I hit the power button and the meters were jumpin', but nothing came out of the speakers. The Fluff looked kinda embarrassed like she didn't want to tell me something.

"You can't hear anything out of the speakers. They must have gotten broken at that party," she said.

Party? Her party, or my party? Which one? When would The Fluff have time for a party when she's always off serving drinks and peanuts to passengers halfway around the world for a living? I can't put my finger on the time when the speakers blew. I mean, when they blew the last time. I've gone to the stereo repair shop more than once in the last few years, that's for sure. But the last time I turned the stereo on, before I conked myself out, I remember it was workin' pretty good. No fuzzy bass...nothin'. So when did they blow? And, I thought, what am I gonna listen to now, that dinky AM radio from the earthquake kit? Or worse, would I have to yak it up with Mom?

The Fluff was always afraid that The Big One would shake our apartment building down or wreck the school when she was out over the ocean somewhere. One night we had a little shaker and she stayed up all night shoving soup cans, toothbrushes, and complimentary airline matchbooks into one of her travel bags just in case The Big One came and knocked the city down like it did in 1906. It never did, but putting that kit together made her drowsy enough to catch a few winks. She was all worried about shakers when she shoulda been more worried about me, I think. Not that I was doing anything that bad. Just kidding again. I've been partying out ever since fifth grade. That's about five years of partying. Maybe things are the way they are because I'm gettin' close to that seven-year-itch thing and it all has to stop because I'm older, who knows.

Dr. Edwards told me that it might take a while before I could put all the pieces together. He came in every day at about 2:00 to check on me. He didn't want to know if I was physically doing okay, because there wasn't anything wrong with my body except a bedsore and maybe I got too skinny when I was out of it, but I told him, "Well, what do ya expect when all you guys do is mainline me this sugar-water junk through a tube? Least you could do is put some flavoring in it or something, I swear." He was just supposed to make sure I didn't have any more "suicidal inclinations." Get that, ha! Suicidal inclinations! I tried to worm my way out of a big mess by goin' out gracefully. . .no muss, no fuss, not even a drop of blood. I didn't splatter myself all over some sidewalk by jumping out of a window onto Market Street. I can just see it now. I'd land on some boring dude in pinstripes like I was a flower pot falling off a window ledge. I'd be smashed flat as a pancake on the cement and he'd be screaming, "My suit! My suit!" So I really thought about it and put together a concoction that would send me off to never-never land so gently that I wouldn't feel it. But I didn't know that The Fluff would get off her flight so early and find me. I also didn't know that swallowing everything I had in my book bag would make me feel so sick before it knocked me out. I do remember that much, at least. And it hurt like you wouldn't believe! Turns my stomach all over again to think about it, really.

That was no so-called "inclination," no way! It was close to a total job. I said close. That's because I can't do anything right. Here I am right back where I started from.

For the longest time, I even thought that my personality was something that wasn't right! Take for instance the way I talk to people. I know I'm kinda blunt and all, but you'd think people would have a sense of humor or somethin'. No way. Everybody has these itty bitty feelings that always seem to get hurt when I say something. But just let Deonna try to use some of my way of talking to people and see what happens!

I remember she told me that one time she went to the can and got surrounded by low-riders. Now if she had done the talkin' like it was herself and not me, she would have taken a pounding from those chicks. But she said she remembered how I talked to them, and so she pushed them around a little bit and guess what? She got outta there without a scratch. Funny thing is, I know she learned something about how to get around in the world from me, but it never crossed my mind for a minute that I should try to talk and act like her. Maybe if I would have tried, things would be different now. For proof, just look at which one of us is stuck in this booby-hatch having to listen to all this nutty garbage from people who only went to school and probably don't even know what kinda life I've been living.

That Edwards, I don't know. I have to see him for an hour every day, rain or shine, until who knows when he decides I'm not gonna reach for the stars anymore. But he keeps asking me if I feel confused. Hell yeah, I feel confused! So I say, "Yeah, I do," and he asks me another question, sometimes like, how do I feel about the other people in my group, or one of those really brainy questions like, "If you were let out of the program right this very minute, what is the first thing you would do?" I tell him any old thing, but in the back of my mind I'm thinkin', hey dude, you SAY I'm not forced to be in here, but the way you put it, it sounds like I'm already in jail. "If" I were let out. Can you even believe it?

He just keeps on scribbling on a scratch pad, whether I talk or not. Edwards' pen is big. Big as one of those disgusting cigars that stink like pig farts. Bigger than his nose even. He's got black hairs growing out of the top of his nose. Get that. Not in his nose, but right on top of his nose. If his nose was a ski slope and you were skiing down it, just before you got to the end of the run you'd smack into the black forest. Didn't his mother ever tell him about tweezers? They should donate his hormones to science, man. Bald man all over the world would sell their limos to buy a gram of his glands, I'm sure.

Maybe I should offer my services, ya know? Be a dealer in cures for baldness. I'm not exactly a pro, but I made a pretty penny selling other stuff that was just as weird. I could even sell stuff that nobody else could unload. Stuff that real Heads wouldn't touch with a ten foot pole I unloaded with hardly a word. There can't be too much difference between bad crack and a shrink's pituitary. Did I spell that right? Who cares. I'm no writer, like I said.

Maybe Edwards will get hold of this banana slug colored notebook and shave his nose, at least. Then on my headstone someone could write that even though I was a big nothing, at least I contributed to making the world a prettier place.

It's hard to see it real clearly, but I kinda remember that once I tried to show off at one of the P.E. classes when we had to do physical fitness testing. If that wasn't acting, like Edwards says, I don't know what is! Man, I was all over that place. Before I ran out to the track, I did up five lines. The thing was gonna start before I was wired up enough, but I ran out there anyway. Just when it kicked in, I felt something go wrong. I was all over that track like a go-cart with bombs for engines, but my heart kept bangin' away like there was a part of it that wanted to break outta my rib cage. It scared me, but I just kept running. I thought, so what if I die? At least I'll show that little jock that there's nothin' wrong with me. Then I conked out. I thought I was gonna die, I swear. When I woke up, that ugly P.E. teacher's whistle was hanging down in front of my eyes and there was Deonna lookin' at me like I was a goner. I don't know how I did it, 'cause I was really sick, but I got up and pretended like I had faked them all out. Then I ran off the track and around the corner to the place behind the store where I made all my buys with Dave. I sat down behind a couple of trash bins and that's the last thing I remember for a long time. When I opened my eyes, there was this big old rat staring at me like I was its dinner. That scared me enough to jump up and run all the way home. I stayed up all night and then crashed for two whole days. Then, when I went to school, I kept hearing strange things in my head. Sometimes that happens, ya know. And now I wonder, did everyone else feel that way too, or was it just me? Was I just completely nuts? Well, maybe I'll never know.

Anyways, the trip back home with The Fluff didn't turn out any different than I thought it would in the first place. She tried to talk to me a little, and I tried to answer, but then I just gave up on the idea because it was like, there I was, practically a grown-up and she didn't even know me! The same thing happened to Deonna, too. She was up on a ladder trying to change a light bulb and her arm was tired from tennis practice. Her mom didn't know her enough to know that the reason she couldn't keep her arm up in the air for very long was not 'cause she was doing dope, but because she was really tired! Can you believe it? Thinking that Deonna Johnson does drugs is so far out that even *I* can't imagine it.

As far as the day back home went, there is just no way my

mom and me could catch up on all the time it took me to get this messed up. Forget it! It was too quiet. We just couldn't get a decent conversation goin'. I could hear the blood sloshing around in my brain, it was so quiet. I'd rather have five tetanus shots than have to go through another day like that as part of the rehab program. Really! I'd rather put up with Edwards and Larry and Lisa the spazz than have to face that again, I swear.

Chapter Five

Alex the Great. Ha. That's what everybody called me in school. You know what was great? Being treated like a star. No matter where I went or what I did, everyone thought I was something else. This one time, I was in a class. I had to go because it was like during the first week and all that, but this teacher, he wanted to have us take a multiple-choice test to find out what level we were at. I think the class had something to do with math, I don't know. I hardly ever knew what class I went to. I just figured that if I showed up to one or the other of them once in a while, that would do the trick. Anyway, he passed out these scan-tron forms and number two pencils, and when he came to me, I said, "No, thank you." Just like that, no thanks, with a brick face and everything. Hey, I was polite but firm, just like my mom was trained to do when some jerk would have too much to drink on the plane and hassle her about getting him one more for the road. I just didn't want to take the test, that's all. So right in front of everybody in the entire room he says, "Well, why not?" I said, "Because why waste the time when I already know I can't answer any of the questions." The teacher just stood there for a minute and didn't say anything. Then he shrugged his shoulders and started passing out the rest of the test stuff. He said, really quiet-like, "I have no answer for you." Then, after class, all these guys came out into the hall and told me how great I was. Someone comes up with Alex the Great and that's that. Everybody wants to hang out with me and copy everything I do. It's a sick world, I'm tellin' ya.

Sometimes I did things just to see how stupid people could get, like the day I took out my old gold and blue kneesock holders from when I used to be in Campfire Girls. I wore one on my right arm to school one day. The next day I saw three other girls wearing the exact same thing on their arms. Can you believe it? If I shoved popcorn in my ears, I bet I would have seen even more of them going along with the program, shovin' as much popcorn in their ears as they could.

At first I thought, well, maybe they're making such a big deal because hardly anyone has red hair. Maybe it's my hair that makes me stick out. Then I thought, no, that's not so special. Maybe it was that I was 5' 4" tall and practically the tallest of all the freshmen girls. I finally decided to stop tryin' to figure it out and take advantage of a good thing. So that's exactly what I did. Now how am I going to tell that to the police officer who keeps callin' my mom up and asking if she'll cooperate and bring me down to the station? He says he knows me from somewhere, which is really the worst, if it's true. But I don't know any cops! So I can't figure out how come he hasn't come in here bustin' down the door if he wants to talk to me. I've seen them do that before on the tube. I bet Edwards keeps saving the day by calling down to the station and telling them that being questioned would make me even more emotionally disturbed than I already am. That busts me up.

Maybe hairy-nose Edwards is right. I'm startin' to remember more as I go along, but my hand is hurting from writing. I'll have to try again later. This isn't so bad, ya know? And what else is there to do, anyway?

In the movies, people are interesting. They say interesting things, they act like they're special, and even if you only hear one or two words that they're saying, you know they're important. I thought that was how it was supposed to be. Like television. Everybody pays attention to you, ya know? It's like this camera is supposed to be following you around except when you don't want it to. That's all I ever wanted. To have somebody with a camera turn it on me full blast and leave it on all day. When I was little, there were these shows where the kid would get into all kinds of trouble, and by the end of a half hour the whole family would be paying attention to him, no matter how bad he mucked things up. It wasn't like I wanted to always be in trouble, but it was the family part that got to me. I don't know what was wrong with my head, but somehow I thought that if I had a camera on me all the time, then out of nowhere this great family would plop down around me and act like they cared about what happened to me. Like for instance, if I was Marsha on that show that had six kids in the same house. Here's how it would go:

"Shhh! Here comes Marsha. She's been up all night crying because this big kid keeps chasing her home after school and trying to beat her up." (That would be one of my sisters at the breakfast table while the maid with the beehive hairdo served up something wholesome like oatmeal and oranges.)

"Why do we have to be quiet?" (The little one would say that.)

"Because, stupid (this would be one of the older brothers talking here), she's really afraid to go to school because Mom and Dad make us wear these stupid-looking shirts with giant collars, and Marsha's afraid they'll make fun of her and beat her up again because she looks like Dumbo the flying elephant."

Then I come downstairs (but in the show, it would really be the middle kid, Marsha, who would play me.). I tell the housekeeper that I'm not feeling so hot. She makes a big fuss over me, and since the folks aren't at home (the mom would be out shopping and would be back in time to see her daily soap operas, and the dad would be doing something really important at his office) she sends me back up to my room, which makes me really happy.

"How come she gets to stay home?" (The little one has a tooth missing and lisps a little).

"Because, stupid, she's Marsha, and this show is all about her, not you."

"Yeah. (This is the other brother talking, the little one with buck teeth.) They don't make TV shows about little punks like you."

Then the housekeeper would make me my own breakfast and bring it up to my room. I would have my own private room, if this were really my show. We'd have a long heart-to-heart talk. Then my TV mom would come home with packages and call up the stairs for help. The TV mom would look ordinary, not like my real mom does. She'd want to know why I was home. The housekeeper would take her into the kitchen so they could talk privately about me. Then the TV mom would sit down and tell me that if it bothered me so much to wear funny clothes to school, we could spend the day shopping for new duds like all the other kids are wearing. Then I would smile and say something stupid if I were really Marsha, like, "You're the greatest mom anyone could ever have."

But this ain't no TV show, that's for sure. In my life, I mean my real life, people do things like rip off booze for their party from a nice guy in a liquor store. It really happened! I remember I was having this party, but I don't remember exactly when I threw it or how it came off, but I needed some good stuff to drink. Deonna said she'd help me out, and we made this great plan for her to take the heat off of me while I helped myself to the goodies in the back of the store. Well, like I said, this is real life, and we got caught. Real life stinks. You'd think you could just nab a few bottles of booze without causin' such a problem, but no way.

In real life, there's no big house with lots of brothers and sisters. Just me, by myself. And it's just me and my mom, The Fluff, who hangs out around the apartment for maybe a day or two when she's not sleeping off jet lag and acts strange around me like she doesn't really know what to say. There's no dad who goes off to work to do something important. There's no dad here at all, and as long as I can remember there never was one. I've seen pictures of this guy who my mom says is my dad, but so what? Where was he when I wanted to learn to ride a bike? And when I was invited to a father's day picnic with the Campfire Girls, where was the father I was supposed to bring with me? Who knows where he is, and who cares anymore, for that matter. It's not like I'm not curious, but why bother to keep asking The Fluff about it? She says, "Well, if he wanted to have a daughter he shouldn't have left in the first place." What do you say to something like that? That just ends the whole conversation right there, in a big loud splat.

I knew my life was no TV show and nobody was following me around all the time to make sure things went okay in a half hour, but that didn't stop me from thinkin' about it all the time. In order to pay the bills, my mom had to work, and since she didn't know how to do anything smart, she had to be either a waitress or a stewardess. Pretty grim. I used to help her pack her bag. And she used to act like it was a really big deal.

When I was in elementary school, other mothers would pick me up and drop me off when my mom was away. I got to stay over a lot at the other kids' houses and do things with them and their families. But I got kinda sick of everybody treating me like I was some poor little thing that they dragged in off the street. I used to sit there and say things like, "It's okay, I like to be alone a lot," when somebody would make a crack about how my mom isn't home because she's working all the time. Then finally I just stopped wanting to go over their houses at all. I'd go home with someone and their mom would be there making something for my friend to eat and acting all interested in what happened at school. And on the weekends, hangin' out in someone's backyard while everybody threw a ball around and barbecued hamburgers and laughed made me feel even worse. I knew that didn't happen for me, and I thought everyone looked at me like I was a charity case.

So what did I do? I stayed at home by myself. I think I spent whole years just hangin' out at school, then going home and lying on the floor listening to music and daydreaming about how things would be someday when I could get everything I wanted. I didn't do anything, just daydream. Until I decided that I couldn't just lie there anymore and that there wasn't a TV camera following me around waiting to see if the show would end and everyone would be happy. I got tough is what I did. I just couldn't wait anymore. And then a bunch of things happened all at once. I'll try to figure it out as I go along. I think everything started happening when I got into high school. Nothing could have started that would have been interesting in elementary school. The school bus picks you up, you sit in the same class, you go to the yard to play, you get back into the bus and it drops you off. You come home, hang out for a while, then go to bed. Then you get up and do it again. That's all. But things changed after junior high, that's for sure, and I can't say I'm glad, looking back on it. What if I never hung out with those guys behind the store? What if I never started liking clothes? And what if I had never met Deonna? It's weird to think like this, but I wonder if I would have tried to kill myself if things were different, or would everything have worked out the same way anyway. Who knows?

Chapter Six

See, even though I met Deonna later on when I got into a fight with that fat chick after school, I first saw her a long time before that, when I was already starting to deal. She didn't know me, and I didn't know her, but every day on my way to the store next to the school, I had to pass by the tennis courts. Sometimes it was so foggy you couldn't see the gates on the other side of the courts, and nobody would be out there except for this black girl, hitting balls so hard that the water from the ground that got on the balls would splat like there were bombs going off inside them. And she'd just keep hittin' 'em when this machine would fling them over the net at her. One day it was really cold, and you could see steam comin' out of the top of her head like she was on fire. It was really something. She was soaking wet and dressed out in white like she was planning on playing a big match, and one of the balls she hit didn't connect just right and flew up and over the high fence. I thought, so what. She's got maybe a hundred balls in that machine. She won't miss this one. But she ran to the fence and looked at me like she wanted a favor. I kept on walking for a minute, but the ball wasn't that far away, so I went over and picked it up and walked back to the court to give it to her. But the gates to the courts were way over on the other side, like I said, and

39

the fence was really high. So I yelled, "Hey, how am I gonna give this thing back?" She told me to just throw it over the top of the fence. I said, "You gotta be kidding. Nobody can throw that high!" Then I tried, but even back then I was skinny and not really strong, and the ball didn't even get near going over the top to her side. I threw the ball down and started to walk away. I wasn't about to humiliate myself just to give this chick back her ball. Then she yelled, "Just do it underhand like this," and she threw another ball over the fence like it was a tiny bowling ball. Well I was pissed by then. Now I'm supposed to chase after another one of her stinkin' balls when I can't even throw straight across much less straight up! So I walked back to the fence and looked her straight in the eye. She was somethin', even then, just to look at. I mean, I was already into all the fashion stuff and I had seen all different body types, but never anyone who had muscles in her arms like Deonna! She didn't look like a guy, either. In fact, it kind of looked nice, especially with all the sweat and drops from the fog everywhere. Deonna had nice eyes, which I noticed right away. They were large and dark brown and it was like you could see just who she was if you kept looking at them, but I didn't want to seem like a nut, so I didn't stare. I said, "Look. You've gotta lot of nerve. Who do ya think I am, your damn dog? I don't fetch for anybody. Get out of your little cage and fetch your own balls." Then I walked away, thinking I had really let her know what's what. Then the next day I had to go back to that spot where I met my guy behind the store for another pick-up. I think even then that I was gettin' all the goodies from Dave. I passed by the courts and there she was again, hitting balls like she was tryin' to kill 'em. I just stood there and watched her, thinking a lot of different things. Like for instance, what's the point of hitting balls back to a machine? And how come she's trying so hard? She saw me standing there and kept hitting them for a minute. Then she switched off the ball machine and walked over to where I was.

"You're Alex, aren't you?" she asked.

"Yeah, so what about it," I said. Everybody in that school knew my name, because I was the one person who everybody knew could get the best dope.

"You want to play sometime? It would be more fun to have someone to hit with instead of this machine."

I thought, was she kidding? Me, Alex Starky, actually hit a ball? And with a racket? I had to concentrate real hard just to make sure I didn't get my legs tangled up most of the time. I said, "You already know I can't throw. What makes you think I can hit?"

"Just thought you might like to try, that's all. It's fun sometimes."

"It's not my thing, if you didn't already know that."

"Yeah, I heard," she said. She looked at me like I ought to know better.

Nobody ever looked at me like that. It almost made me feel like I was really doing something bad, when I had convinced myself that I was only doing what I had to do to get along. "Too bad for you, huh?" she said.

I wanted to get in there and smack her. How dare she think that what she was doing was any better than what I did? There's no way she can be so high and mighty now, though. She's done things I bet she'd never want to tell anyone. Like lying to a cop and helpin' me rip off booze. But back then I didn't have any friends, and she seemed like she wouldn't laugh if I messed up, so I kinda backed off and told her that what I did was just for fun money, and no thanks, I was all thumbs when it came to sports. My body just grew all of a sudden, and when it did I couldn't control it very well. I drop things a lot. So I never got into playing catch, or even volleyball. It was too embarrassing.

See, I stand pretty tall next to everybody else, and wherever I go my hair and my body are like a neon sign that says,

"Look at me." Well, isn't that the pits? The last thing a dealer wants is to stand out in a crowd. But I managed okay. Then we yakked a little bit, even though I was late to meet Dave. I knew I would never play tennis with Deonna. She was just too good, and she wasn't, you know, sort of afraid of me like the other kids were. She seemed like the kind of person who would tell you that you had something stuck in your teeth when everybody else would be too embarrassed. So I bet she would tell me how out of whack and clumsy I was the first time I even tried to hit one of her tennis balls. Anyhow, that's how she knew who I was before I got into that fight with that turd Zoila.

Once you start dealing, you can never tell why people like you. I never trusted anyone. But Deonna was different. She never got high. And because she didn't want anything that I had, it was okay to be real with her. I had nothin' to lose, and neither did she. Well, I guess that's not true now. It might have been better if I really did kill myself. Then Deonna wouldn't have to explain what she was doing hanging around with me. It makes me feel like some kinda curse, and it's just too bad because who knows what she thinks of me now.

Chapter Seven

A little while ago Larry peeked into my room, which is really weird because he never came near my side of the hall before.

"Alex? You okay?"

"What's up, man. Is this like an honor or something?" I asked. I was sittin' on my bed about to write in the banana-slug notebook when he stuck his head inside my door.

"Well, I heard your friend and you talking before dinner and you sounded kind of upset," Larry said.

"That's right, I am upset. I am real upset," I said, and gave him a signal to come in. He might as well. Looks like we'd be stuck in this program together for ages anyway. No sense makin' it worse than it already was.

Larry sat down on one of the two chairs in the corner. My room was pretty small, but they made it feel like home as much as they could. Home was never any big deal to me anyway. Doesn't matter whether it's here, with the table and chairs, TV and bed, or the apartment with the Fluff. It's just a place to flop, right? Except now there's no hope.

"You don't have to tell me, you know. I mean, I don't want to be nosy or anything, but you guys sounded like you were really going to duke it out there for a while."

I never wanted to talk to anyone in this program, especially Larry. I figured that if I was gonna get through this, I'd just keep quiet and let the time go by, then get Deonna to spring me outta here. But that's not gonna happen anymore, and I'm just plain stuck. Why not talk to Larry? There wasn't anyone else, that's for sure.

"It's like this," I told Larry, who really didn't look as scuzzy as I thought once I took a close-up shot of him, "I have this friend, or at least I thought I did, and me and her, we were real tight. I was gonna stick it out here until she could help me out. But today she said a bunch of things and now I don't know which end is up."

Deonna was sitting just about where Larry was. We got over all the hellos and how-are-yous and all that, and I couldn't listen to most of the junk she was tellin' me, like how she wanted me to be at the tryouts for the team next week and all that.

"Let's get down to the real dirt here," I said to her.

"That *is* real dirt to me," she said. She had a funny look on her face like her feelings were hurt. That was somethin' new! It used to be that I could say anything I wanted to Deonna. She wouldn't care. She would just listen, like nothing I said would ever bother her.

"But this is an emergency, Deonna. I've got two choices in front of me. I can either stick it out here for who knows how long, and believe me, this is a real funny farm, or else I can skip out, go back to living with the Fluff, and she'll stick me in Wintersburg."

"You're kidding! Wintersburg? You won't make it in there, Alex. You're not the type," Deonna said.

"My mom's already checked it out. There's this cop that's been harassing her. Says he knows me and he's just waiting until I get out to talk to me about something. What it is, I don't know, and as of right now I could care less. But if I get out of here and go home, I wind up on probation because I'm a first-time offender. That means Wintersburg, loud and clear."

"You mean you don't know why he wants to see you at all?" Deonna looked at me like I was some kinda nut case.

"No. Why should I care? Maybe he wants to give me a corny talk about why drugs are bad for you and all that. Or tell me what the law says about people who try to commit suicide or something. Like I said, so what. I only care about one thing right now. I've gotta get out!"

"Well," Deonna said, like she was worried about what I just said so she changed the subject, "so why don't you stay in here? Maybe it will do some good for you."

"You've got to be kidding, man. Me? Here? Do you know what goes on here? No, you don't. You're out in the sunshine every day playin' with little green balls, like an angel. You don't have to sit here and listen to this crud like I do. These guys are real strange, I tell ya."

Deonna's face was like a brick, I swear. She said, "But you've got a problem. People who try to kill themselves need to figure out what's going on and do something about it. It's not right any other way."

"Don't tell me what I need! How would you know? You've got it all sewn up. You get out of school, and there's college. And you have two parents to take care of everything for you. But me. . .well, it's not the same. What I need is to get out of here. I mean completely. Like out of town. Start fresh somewhere else. I don't need this jibber-jabber. These rap groups are driving me nuts! Sometimes I feel like what they're tellin' me is makin' sense. That's how bad it is!"

"Maybe you should listen if it makes sense," she said.

"Hey, whose side are you on, anyway? I need you right now, man. I need you to get me out of here! This is no joke, Deonna. I need some cash, some clothes, and maybe even someone who can say, 'You're doin' the right thing. Everything will be okay.' But instead, you think I should stay right here. You know what? It makes me wonder what you're all about anyway. Maybe I shouldn't have trusted you these last two years. Maybe you're a narc, who knows?"

"I am not a narc. What are you getting all worked up about, Alex? I'm still your friend. But I've been doing a lot of thinking, especially while you were in a coma..."

"I was not, I repeat, NOT in no coma!"

"You were. That's what you call it when you go into limbo for three weeks and don't wake up or respond to outside stimuli," she said.

"Outside stimuli, my foot! You've been talkin' to that hairy beast, haven't you?"

"What hairy beast? You don't have to yell, you know."

"Edwards! That's who!"

"Look, Alex, I didn't come here to fight with you. I came to see how you're doing. When you were...well, out of it, I came every day that I could. I wished you would wake up. I thought about how great it would be if you'd wake up and stop all the drug stuff. Maybe you could make something of yourself after all. I missed talking to you and hanging out with you. Even when we were doing something wrong, it was nice to know we were tight. Then one day I came to visit after you woke up, and they told me you were in the rehabilitation program and that it would be better if I stayed away, so I did. I thought it would be good for you to sort of clean out your head. Take my Uncle Ray, for instance. He's an alcoholic, but finally he got some help, and now he doesn't drink any more. He's running all over the States with my Aunt Martha having a second honeymoon, because the first time around he didn't even know he had gotten married."

"Oh, that uncle of yours. He gave you nothin' but trouble. He'll drink again, I know it like I know my own name. If it's anything like what's happened to me, he'll always wanna get loaded."

"Maybe that's so. He's already blown it once. But then he went right back to AA and started over. He sends us letters all the time about it. He says the trick is never to give up on yourself. He says that it's really hard to face things sober, but it always turns out to be worth the trouble. And I don't care about all those times he woke us up in the middle of the night. If you could have seen him before he took off on his honeymoon, you'd think just like I do and forgive him. He said that he had to kill the part of himself that kept taking control over his whole life, even when it was against his will. And he did it, at least in his own head. It gave him a second chance to change things. And my Uncle Ray is no young guy, either. You've got lots of time to enjoy life, Alex. Everybody should get another chance. I thought maybe they were teaching you something like that here. But I don't know. You don't seem too happy."

"If you were here, you wouldn't be either," I said. "Just do me one more favor, puhleeeze? Pretty please? I swear I'll pay you back some day. Help me get out of here and I'll. . ."

"You'll what? Wind up in jail somewhere? Or dead this time? Or kill. . ." Deonna stopped talking like she had to keep from saying something else.

"Kill schmill. Look. Let's kill the sermon, okay? It's like this: I've got $250 in stash under my bed in a shoebox. I've got an old backpack and a sleeping bag from my Campfire Girl days in my bedroom closet. School won't be in for a little while yet, so you don't have to worry about ditching during the day. You could get in there and grab the stuff when the Fluff's not around. Then everything would be great! Don't ditch out on me when I really need a friend now. It's not right. I've always been right there when you needed me, man. No questions asked and all that. Just remember the good times, will ya?"

"I think I better be going now," Deonna said.

"You can't! I'm stuck here, why don't you get that through

your thick skull!" I shouted. But Deonna got up and started to walk out of my room into the hall. Then she turned around and looked at me like she felt sorry for me or something.

"This isn't easy to say, Alex, but what's right for me is not up to you anymore. And I know that to be a good friend I've got to do some things that maybe you won't like, such as not helping you to get out of here so that maybe you'll get better. Next week, like I told you, I'm trying out for the team. I asked outside if you could come and watch, and that guy Sam said as long as your doctor says okay and if your mom goes with you, you could go. I'd like you to be there. It would mean a lot to me. I'm playing a few of the older girls, and I'm up against the worst odds. You know that they don't like me and they don't want me on the team, so it's going to be tough to work my way up the ladder and wipe them out one by one. If I had a loud rooting section, maybe it would cover up the booing. That means you and your mom and my parents. See if you can make it."

Larry's mouth was kinda hanging open when I told him all this. "So Deonna just turned around and walked out, huh?"

"Yep. Just like that. Just like we were never pals. And I was just sittin' here thinkin' about the time I covered for her. I didn't let her down when she was in trouble, ya know."

"How's that?" Larry put his foot up on the chair to make himself more comfortable.

I thought to myself, why should I talk to him? He tried to booby-trap me in the Workroom when we played Hot Seat. He's a mess. But then I thought, well, the heck with it. Who else is there to talk to? And he really seems kinda interested, ya know? Go ahead. Maybe he's not such a bad guy after all.

"Well, see, this one time I was gonna have a party. A really big wingding with good sounds and the place jammed with great people. The only thing was that I had to get some party juice. Well, Deonna said she would help me out. Turns out she didn't know that we couldn't just walk into any old store and actually buy the stuff. But she decided to go along with the program anyhow, and we made up a plan how we'd slip into this liquor store and she'd throw the counter guy off the scent while I padded my book bag. But when she was off talkin' to him, I was in the back tryin' to decide just which stuff to get. So dumb old me, I opened up one of the bottles for a quick taste. This cop jumped out of nowhere and grabbed it right outta my face!"

"Then what happened?" Larry asked.

"Oh, nothin' much. The cop tried all these scare tactics on me. But ya know, the one thing that worried me is that he asked me for all this information. I thought, oh no, if I tell him the truth we're done for. So I told him I went to a different high school and he took it all down. Whatta goober. Then, before he let me go, he asked if me and Deonna knew each other. Well, I knew if I said yes, or even looked at her like I knew her, she'd be in just as much trouble as I was. See, she has these great plans to be a big tennis star, and if somethin' goes wrong while she's in high school it could wipe out her chances. So it's kinda like I saved her career. And now this. How could she just walk out on me like that? And how could she compare me with that drunk of an uncle of hers? She thinks Heads are like slime-wad gutter drunks. No way! It's scary when ya think of how she's changed in just a few weeks, and I haven't."

"Boy, you can say that again," Larry said.

"What are ya gettin' at?" I asked.

"You're something else, Alex. Lisa and Sam and Janine and me have all tried to get through to you. And you act like this whole thing is some kind of a big joke. You act like we're the ones who have the problem, but not you, you're just in here for kicks or something. But you know what? The three of us are in here because we all did the exact same thing at the exact same time. And you don't see Lisa trying to escape, do you? No. Even though she's all messed up, she's at least trying to fix things. Look here." Larry pulled up the sleeve on his shirt. There was a big scab and a gash across his left wrist.

I waved my hands at him to push his sleeve back down and closed my eyes. There was just something about seeing the spot where blood once gushed out that reminded me of something so gross and gnarly that I started to feel sick to my stomach.

"When her parents come on Friday, you bet they're going to see a change in Lisa, even if you don't. You didn't know how far Lisa had already come by the time they put her in the rehab program. But she jumped off her roof head first! She would have died, but when she jumped part of her body hit a rain gutter, so she didn't hit as hard as she planned to. That's why, besides being an addict, her body's all messed up. And look at her now, Alex. She's alive and trying. We are both trying because we know we have to. We know we're not perfect. And even if you sit in here until you rot, you're the type of person who's the worst off of all of us, no matter how much help people try to give you."

"Hey, what is this? I open my guts a little bit and you step all over 'em!" I thought, he's doin' it again! He's out to get me, the little paranoid!

Larry stood up and went for the door. "Why don't you give it a chance, Alex? What's so bad about being who you really are instead of a block of cement like you pretend to be. I know you think Lisa is a full-on MR, and you probably think I'm worse than that. But at least we're trying to do a little better, and that's a lot more than anyone can say about you. You're doomed!" Then he ran out the door.

Chapter Eight

Edwards came in to see me this morning. As usual, nobody had told him that his nose needed a shave. He plunked himself down at the table like he did every day, and I just stared at his arm hairs and tried to count them while he talked.

"Happy Thursday, Alex. You've been here long enough to know how our sessions are structured. Why don't you start by telling me how your visit with your friend went yesterday?"

"I don't wanna talk about it, if ya don't mind," I said.

"Why not? Did something go wrong? Did you have a falling out of sorts?" Edwards must have some new kid on his schedule, I thought, because he had a brand new yellow notebook with him. Mine was totally thrashed.

"Well yeah, it kinda didn't go too good," I said. I just felt tired when I got up that morning, like I was beat and out of tricks. Since Deonna wouldn't help me, since I didn't have even one friend on the face of the earth, why bother? I was down, man. What good would it do to fight Edwards off, or any of them, for that matter? Let 'em have what they wanted. They wanted to see me eat it, that's what. Well, my face is in it now, I said to myself. Might as well have mud pie for dessert!

"Ummm. Well, let's go with that a bit." Edwards pulled his big cigar-shaped pen out of his pocket and flipped the top of his note pad over and started scribbling. I tried to read it upside down but it was too much trouble. It was like I just didn't have the energy.

"I kinda feel like I'm alone. I don't know how to put it. I mean, I never thought that before. Before, I always had everybody on my side. Now it's like I can't even get these loony-tunes in here to like me."

"Being liked is important to you, is it?" Edwards said.

"It probably is to you, too. How would you like it if you were nothin'? If you had no brains and couldn't do anything and everything you did turned out to be a stupid flop?"

"Why do you think that happens to you?"

"I don't know. I wish I did. I don't know anything anymore," I said. It's true. I felt like there was just no hope for me. Here I was with all these big plans and they all fell apart. Like that last party I had. I know I can remember now that I had it, but what happened there is kinda fuzzy. I remember that I kept going over to the stereo and adjusting the bass and treble, because the speakers were turned up so high that they were about to bust. I think I even remember one of them blowin', but I'm not sure about that. I know that Deonna was there, and that Dave and Rabbit and me were in my room basin', but then it comes to me like something gnarly happened. It seems kinda half real and half like I'm imagining it, but sometimes when I think back I'm driving my mom's car. Then I think, well okay, but where did I get her keys? I never had a set, and The Fluff never let me take the car out before then. It just doesn't make sense. Nothing does. First I wake up in a hospital and can't figure out why I'm there, and then when I try to get out so I can make something of myself, I can't even do that.

"Oh, I think you know far more than you give yourself credit for knowing, Alex." Edwards' eyes crinkled up in a smile. He said, "If you would only see that you're in complete charge of everything you do, then instead of reacting to all the things that you do wrong, you could start letting the bad things go by the wayside and begin acting instead of reacting."

"I don't get what you're sayin'," I said, but I wanted to know. It sounded kinda interesting.

"Let's say you do something you're sorry for. Instead of covering it up, you decide to just let it go and start fresh. Let's say you make the same mistake five times in one day. It wouldn't matter, if you would just let it go. That would free you up to concentrate on the things that you felt you did right."

"Well, I can tell ya right now, there isn't one thing I've done right in a long, long time. First, I wanted to be a clothes designer when I got out of high school. But I wasn't that great of a student, ya' know? So I figured, forget it. Then I figured out a way to make money, and I thought I'd stash it away so I could go to a design school when I graduated. But somehow that didn't work out, either. Anyway, I liked having friends, so I kinda forgot about everything else. And now I have no friends. I'm such a jerk. I even ask favors that are way out of whack." I thought, let this guy figure a way out of this!

"I've spoken with your mother, and she tells me that you're very talented in fact. Not that some of the clothes you've put together are to my taste, but from what she described, it shows great imagination, incredible originality. The world is always ready for a grand helping of that," he said.

"What good would it do me now? I don't even have a sewing machine. I was saving up to buy one. I've got $250 at home, but I can't get to it."

"You want to sew, eh? What else would you need?" Edwards really seemed interested. He wrote down "sewing machine" on his pad.

"A pile of old-lady jewelry, lots of throw-away clothes. You know, the stuff you stick in the garage and never wear. I want to make stuff that's incredible out of nothing."

"Let's say I found a way to put a machine and some of what you asked for in here. Could you make something of it?"

"Heck, yeah! What're ya sayin'? Would you do that for me?" I thought, is this guy for real, or is he just baiting me into telling him something?

Edwards stood up. He was really a tall guy. Funny thing, when you look up at him, you can't see the hairs on his nose. In fact, he wasn't bad lookin' at all. "Let me see what I can come up with. I think I know where I can get a used machine. The old clothes will be easier to get than you think. I'll come by tomorrow afternoon, after the session with the parents."

"You're serious?" I asked.

"I am if you are," he said, then he walked to my door and added, "I brought you a new notebook. Do you want it?"

"Sure. But do you think I could also have one that doesn't have lines on it? I mean, like for drawing and stuff? And maybe a few pencils to go with it?"

"I'll see what I can dig up for you, Alex." Then Edwards smiled and walked away.

As soon as he left, I flopped on my bed and thought, okay. So I'm reacting instead of acting. Well, if Edwards really comes through, I'm gonna start acting like you never saw anyone act in your life! I couldn't believe it! A real sewing machine! It would be weird because I'd have to teach myself how to make it work, but really, how hard could it be? Lots of people work machines like that and somehow the clothes get made. Then I thought about what I'd make. Too bad I didn't have anything to work on right then. I'd make something faster than you could boil water. My head was spinning with ideas about all the stuff I always wanted to put together, like this shirt I've always had in mind. Kind of a new idea, where you could rip off pieces of it here and there, and then button it back together real fast like if it got cold. Maybe sometimes you'd want to wear it with the sleeves up, and other times you could pull the sleeves down. With leather you'd want to have it like that because leather costs a lot and it's a pain to buy all different kinds of leather things because they're only good for certain times. Maybe one where you could change the collar or turn it inside out. One side would be one color and the other side would be black and mean looking. Or pockets that hung on the outside of a skirt that you could see into, made out of something like fish-netting. I could do that! And I would too, if Edwards would only come though.

I thought, please, if nothing else ever happens to me, let it happen like he said just this one time. Then I would really go for it, no joking around.

I flipped through the new yellow notebook. I wondered what I was going to put in it. It wasn't like I had to use it or anything, but they give you a lot of free time in this program and sometimes you just don't want to watch TV or walk around outside in the patio or garden area. Sometimes I would just lie on my bed writing down any old junk. Then I'd stick it inside my pillowcase so it would be hard to find. The old banana slug notebook was a wreck. I had made part of it into a tree by folding down the pages and standing it up on its side. I had ripped half pieces off of it and made tiny paper airplanes. Sometimes when I was mad I scribbled so hard that the pen went all the way through three sheets of paper at a time.

A couple of times I put a few lines in it from songs that I knew. My old friend Rabbit had turned me on to all the words on the back of his Joni Mitchell albums, and I used to know all of them. But now when I tried to think of what they were, I only got a line or two and I knew they were out of order. I thought, boy, you sure are a mess if you can't remember stuff you used to sing even when you were so high you couldn't walk! But the ones that always gave me the goose bumps I wrote down over and over again, to try and get back the rest of the words. So I tried it again. I got the same couple of lines.

"It's coming on Christmas
They're cutting down trees..."

And then, wow, I got two more lines, just like that!

"I wish I had a river
I could skate away on."

So I figured, if I could get back just those two extra lines, I could probably remember everything. That's what I thought I'd use the new notebook for. No more making happy faces and then crossing out the eyeballs so hard that there were big holes in the pages behind it. No more writing the same cuss words over and over again, no way. I had some good ideas once, about how I was gonna make this or that getup, and I can't remember what they were, even though I used to be able to close my eyes, especially right in the middle of a boring class, and see every seam, every zipper, and every color of bead I wanted to sew onto it. If I'm gettin' a machine, I've gotta remember all of it, or like Larry says, I'm doomed.

What I didn't tell Edwards was about Deonna. I want to tell him to see what he'd say about someone you once thought was your friend, but someone who kicks you when you're really down. I mean, can you believe it? This chick thinks she's really hot stuff or something. She never pulled that "holier than thou" stuff on me before, or I would never have let her hang out with me! Deonna always treated me like I was another normal everyday person. She never looked at me like I was some freak or something, like I know everybody else did. Who cares about everyone else? And now I'm stuck in this place for sure.

If it weren't for that machine, I'd skip outta here right now, without food, or clothes, or my sleeping bag, or my stash money. Who needs it? But before anything else happens, I want to give it a try. Just once I want to see if I can do it. I mean, maybe I should go to Wintersburg if I can't make something really special happen.

Anyway, I can't go on lettin' Deonna Johnson think she's something and I'm nothin'. It's not like she wanted to get rid of me for good, ya know. She said I could go to her tennis thing if my mom would go. Well, I'll be seeing the Fluff tomorrow for parents' day. She probably won't want to go. The Fluff hates sports. That's probably why I don't like sports either. Maybe there's something to it.

Well, it's time to go to the Workroom for another wonderful session of psycho games.

Chapter Nine

I can't even believe it, man. Today it was like miracles happened. Real live miracles. It was like how you feel when you're lucky enough to catch sight of a rainbow when it's raining somewhere else and the sun is out, only instead of just one rainbow, you see two. Except today was better than that. I can't sleep until I get this out. This is better than the best high I've ever had. And it's not that giant things happened like winning a million dollars. It's just that a bunch of little things happened all at once. Today things have definitely changed. Aya!

What happened is that after breakfast I came back to my room to scribble around in my notebook, but I was kinda bored so I turned on the TV. I nearly flipped by the public station, but I got a quick look at this talk show about new fashions and so I flopped into one of the chairs and just left it on. They had some outrageous stuff and they were showing it like it was a fashion show and people could bid on the stuff by calling a toll-free number. I thought I heard someone behind my back, but I didn't wanna miss even one second of the show, so I ignored it.

Just when I saw this great dress that looked like a giant silk shirt with all the embroidery on the arms and collar, I heard a voice say, "Wow." I turned around, and there was

Lisa standing there all lopsided like she is. She had just walked into my room and started watching the show. I don't know why, but instead of being mad at her for barging in on me, I said, "Is that a killer dress or what?"

"Wish I could call that number at the bottom of the screen," she said. I pushed one of the chairs toward her and she sat down next to me.

"That's nothin'," I said, "I've worn stuff that was ten times better than that."

"You make clothes?"

"Well, not yet, but soon. Here," I said, pushing my notebook with some of my drawings toward her, "feast your eyes on this!"

She flipped through a few of the pages. "I didn't know you were into this."

"This is my life, man. You don't know anything about this part of it."

Lisa kept looking at one of my drawings that was kind of like what one of the models was wearing on TV that we both liked. "If I had a figure like hers, I could make this dress look fantastic!"

I couldn't believe it. Except for the half of her body that kinda fell down, Lisa was already prettier than any model I had ever seen. She could get a job modeling clothes any day of the week, even with her body problems and everything.

"What's with you? You've got a body that's a zillion times better than those goobers on the tube."

Lisa kinda turned a little red and said, "Oh, yeah. And diamonds fall out of my mouth when I speak, too."

"Don't you think you're pretty?" I asked.

"No," she said. She looked at me like I was a crazed weirdo. "Nobody's ever told me that. You're the first one."

"That's nuts, man! Don't your folks tell you, or don't you look in the mirror once in a while? I mean chicks at my school would die flat out if they looked even half as good as you do. You'd probably look great if you just woke up bald and covered with mud."

"How come you're telling me all this, Alex? I thought you'd scream at me for sneaking into your room. But when I saw that dress I couldn't help it. You never even talked to me before."

"I'm tellin' ya, Lisa, it's true. And here, look at this one here." I flipped forward a few more pages into the note-book, skipping a few pages where I wrote private stuff. I especially didn't want her to see the newest pages where I started remembering that I really did take my mom's car out for a joy ride after that last party. I knew Dave was in that car and I kept seeing red all over the place when I thought about it, but if what I thought turns out to be true, I really wouldn't want the spazz to get wind of it. That would do her in for good, even though she didn't seem like a spazz anymore. Funny. Soon as I pictured her in a fashion show wearin' one of my creations, she looked like a normal girl. Am I losin' my mind, or what?

"Wow. That's great! I'd give anything to be able to wear something like that. Anything!"

"You could, ya know. I could put that one together for you in about a day. Well, maybe a few days, 'cause I don't really know how to work a sewing machine yet, but I will soon."

"You've really got a lot of talent. I wish I had talent like that. You're lucky. You can really draw, too," Lisa said.

"Are you kiddin' me or what? Who needs talent when you've got looks like yours? All you have to do is sit back and let the money roll in. You could have your face on the cover of magazines, man. No joke."

"You think so? I don't get it. Nobody else says so."

Lisa had left my door open, and we both jumped when it flew all the way open and then in walks Edwards with this giant packing box, and he's breathing hard like he's just run a marathon or somethin'.

"You're in luck, Alex," he said, as he put the box down

on the floor. "Yesterday after I left here I visited one of my friends out in Daly City. She always has a garage full of junk that she says someday she'll donate to Saint Anthony's. I told her I was looking for a sewing machine for one of my patients, and voila! Here's what we came up with."

Edwards bent over into the packing box and grunted as he pulled out an old sewing machine. A little sweat splashed on the black base of the machine as he leaned over to pull it out of the box and put it on the table. It was covered with dust and looked like it had seen better days.

"Wow. You get your own sewing machine?" Lisa asked, and then started twitching. I ignored it. Who cares about a little spazz attack now and then?

"You mean this is mine?" I asked Edwards.

"It's all yours. You can take it with you when you leave here." He pulled a handkerchief out of his back pocket and wiped the sweat off his face.

"Hah," I snorted, "that means never."

"Nope, that means check-out time is Monday noon," he smiled.

"I'm outta here? Is this some kinda bad joke? 'Cause if it is..." I just couldn't believe it. Not to see this little hospital room, not to have to hang around with nurses and shrinks, well, I couldn't believe it!

"Today is parents' day for a reason. You, Lisa, and Larry are all going home at the same time. We have a special couple of sessions scheduled to go this weekend up at the Russian River that should arm you with enough inspiration to get you through the transition. And you'll be coming to see me separately and together quite frequently once you all get settled into real life at home."

Lisa looked worried. "Dr. Edwards, what if we don't think we're ready yet?"

"I'm afraid the decision has already been made. We know it will be scary to go back to the same surroundings that have contributed to your troubles in the first place, but you can't hide out here forever. Besides, the unfortunate truth is that your places are being filled with overdose survivors who may not fare as well as the three of you have." Edwards put away his handkerchief and told us he'd see us Monday morning.

"Hey, Dr. Edwards," I called out into the hallway after him, "is all this for real?"

"It's for real," he called back over his shoulder.

"We're gettin' outta here, we're gettin' outta here," I sang as I jumped around and held onto the top of the sewing machine like it was a gym bar or somethin'.

"Well, I'm glad for you, at least. You've got a lot to look forward to," Lisa said, and stood up to go.

"Hey, where ya goin'? I'm gonna take this old banged-up piece of junk and make you anything in this notebook you like," I said.

"Well, it's time to go to the Workroom," she said, like she didn't hear me. Then I guess everything dawned on her all at once. "Anything in this book? Whatever I want? What if my parents won't let me wear it?"

"Why wouldn't they?" I asked.

"Wait until you meet my parents today. Then you'll know why," she said, flipping through the pages. She stopped back at the one I showed her that looked somethin' like the one on the TV fashion show. "Can you really make this one for me? Even if they don't let me wear it, at least I can keep it in my closet for when you get famous. I can say I've got an original."

"It's yours, Lisa. This incredible Alex the Great masterpiece will be all yours."

"We better go, we're going to be late," Lisa said. Before we got around to the other side of the building where the Workroom was, she said, "Hey, Alex, how come you're so different all of a sudden? You're kind of nice, but nobody would ever know it before today, you know."

I opened the door for Lisa and said, "Because today, well, today there's hope."

Chapter Ten

Sitting around in a small circle in the Workroom were Lisa's parents, my mom, Sam, Janine, Dr. Edwards, and Larry's father. We sat down on the arms of an old easy chair next to everybody.

"Nice to have you with us," Larry whispered. We were late, but I could care less. I was too stoked over the sewing machine and knowing that no matter what, I was gettin' as far away from this hospital as I could.

Dr. Edwards announced that we were all to leave on Monday and that this session was to give us a chance to talk with the counselors and each other about how we would handle our lives once we got back home. He said that it would be hard on us, but it would be difficult for the parents, too.

"What could be difficult about having little Lisa back with us again? We'll just go lickety split back to how things were before this entire fiasco began. Everything will be just fine," Lisa's mother said.

I could see right then and there what Lisa meant about her parents. They looked like those two people in that picture of the old American farming husband and wife with the pitchfork and the overalls. No way were they going to let her wear an Alex the Great creation! She was right. And what did they know about Lisa? Nothing! What her mom said told me that they were a pair of goobers before and they'd still be that way once Lisa got home. Sometimes when you come down too hard on a person's spirit, they go just the opposite way that you want 'em to. That's probably what happened to Lisa, and she overdosed because of it. And Lisa's mom was the kind of person who you could tell had an ego the size of two planets. She wasn't very pretty; her face was hard and pasty, just like a brick with flour smeared all over it. She'd never be as pretty as Lisa, even if she tried for the rest of her life. And that's why Lisa didn't think she was pretty. Her mom wanted to be the star. Well, I think that if Lisa keeps comin' here for pep talks with Edwards, maybe she'll look in the mirror one day, and even though her face is a little bit off, she'll see that she's really something else. I'm stayin' in touch with her after we get outta here, that's for sure.

Larry's dad was this big macho type of a guy. Right in the middle of Sam's talk about how we could look at our addictions like they were little kids living inside of us telling us what to do even though we didn't want to, Larry started to cry. His dad just sat there, chewing on his dentures and looking at the wall like he didn't want to see any of it.

"I'm afraid it's going to happen again. I don't want it to. I'm not ready to leave yet," he said, cryin' like he used to in our old Workroom meetings.

Edwards made him feel a little better, and Sam came across the room and gave Larry a big hug and told him everything would be okay, and still that father of his just sat there like it wasn't happening.

Finally he said, "Larry's a good man. He'll get a grip soon enough."

Can you believe it? The guy's an ice machine! What's gonna happen to Larry once he's alone with this guy? I'd give anything to meet his mom. She wasn't there because she was gettin' things ready for Larry at home. I can just picture his bedroom covered with wall-to-wall pictures of military junk like guns and swords and five star generals. Even though I'm crazed about gettin' outta here, I'm kinda sorry I don't have just a day or two more so I could find out more about Larry. I don't know if I would have ever liked him, 'cause he's just not my type, ya know? But I'm kinda curious to see what happens with him.

Then, there's me. Alex Starky. And my mom, who doesn't look at all like The Fluff anymore. She didn't look much better than the last time I saw her when she took me home for the day. We went around the room and everybody said something about what kind of a son or daughter they were and how they wanted to be. The parents had to do the same thing. It came around to me and my mom's turn. I never knew she was the type who got embarrassed, but she was blushing so hard that her face matched the red blouse she had on.

"I'm not very good at talking in public like this, but I just want to say, well, I'm very proud of Alex and so happy that she's come through this so well. We have a long way to go after she comes home. I just want, more than anything else, to get to know her and let her know that no matter who she turns out to be, I'll love her and support her and make her proud to have me for a mother. That's all I have to say."

I'm no crybaby, never have been. But when she said that to everybody in the room, it was like rockets goin' off in my eyeballs, ya know? I couldn't believe it! First the sewing machine, then getting to go home, and now this! It was just too much. My mom wanted to know who I was. She wasn't like that before. All I ever wanted was to have someone around who cared, and now she's sayin' that she's the one. That's what I think I meant when I said that today was like seein' a double rainbow when you're not even gettin' rained on. I knew right then and there that no matter how hard it was to get started, I was gonna learn how to be nice to my mom. If she was gonna try, then so was I. Monday at

Deonna's tryouts would be somethin' else, man. Just me and her watching someone I liked...together. How weird, but how nice!

The weekend at the River was pretty intense. We did things like role playing, and watched a few videos about what physically happens to you when you crave your favorite drug. The rest of the time, we talked our heads off. Monday came faster than I thought it would, and I kinda felt just a little bit scared about my mom comin' to get me and everything. Here things are goin' so well and I just didn't want to wreck it. This was my big chance to do somethin' good with my life. I really thought I could make it.

Then my mom came to pick me up. We went straight from the hospital to the courts at school. At first my mom and I didn't really know what to say to each other, and it felt kinda squirmy. But we kept tryin'. By the time we got to the courts, which was a little early, we were yakking away about stuff we remembered from way back. I was amazed because I could remember all kinds of stuff we used to do that I couldn't think of not too long ago. Then I saw the store next to the school, and then the parking lot next to the courts, and I got these nasty feelings like somethin' was hangin' over my head, somethin' gnarly and gross and scary.

Deonna came running up to us before we even got to the bleachers.

"You're really here! I didn't think you'd make it, but I'm so happy you did!" she said. She was nice to my mom and showed her where she could sit. She had taped two pieces of cardboard with our names on them in the front row, right next to Mr. and Mrs. Johnson. My mom went to say hello to them, and Deonna and I stayed back outside the gates for a little bit.

"You look sort of different," Deonna said.

"It's been a real trip, I tell ya. But I am different," I said.

"Nothin's ever gonna be the same."

"That's good to hear. I thought you were a goner there for a while."

"I was. But not anymore, man. I figured out a few things about myself that I didn't know before, and that makes the whole deal more in my favor," I said.

"Speaking of deals, well, I don't know how to tell you this, but I saw Dave's dad up in the bleachers." Deonna pointed to him, and right away I knew that he had somethin' to do with the nasty feelin' I had when we passed the store. Then I started remembering more and more, like a whole movie passed right before my eyes in a split second. I kinda choked up, right in front of Deonna.

"Are you okay?" she asked.

"I guess so. It's just that while I was up at camp I had this nightmare that Dave got killed in a car accident and it was all my fault. Then I woke up, but the nightmare didn't go away. Just now I looked at that guy up there and I remembered everything. He's probably gonna want to talk to me, isn't he?"

"Probably. But it's been a while since that happened, just remember that. You've changed, and he'll see that it wasn't all your fault if he talks to you. And besides," Deonna looked down at the ground like she was ashamed of herself or somethin', "I have to tell you something else, but I don't think you're going to like it very much."

"What's that?"

"Remember when I visited you in the hospital when you first woke up?"

"Nope."

"Don't you remember anything I said at all just before you opened your eyes?"

"Come on, you know I was veggin' out. How could I know you were yakkin' at me?" I said.

"Well, it's too bad you can't remember it, but I'll tell you a little of what I said. I told you that I couldn't hang around and watch your mom worry about what happened to you, and that even though I promised that I wouldn't say anything, I'd have to break my promise. It wasn't easy to do, but I learned something out of it," Deonna said.

"Out of what?"

"Out of the whole thing. . . everything that happened to us since the first day I saved you from Zoila. I figured out that sometimes, when you really care for someone, you do whatever you have to do to help them out, even if means doing something that person might not like."

"So what did ya do?" I asked.

"I told your mom," Deonna said, "then I went down to the police station and talked to Officer Kingsley about you. He knows everything. We spent two hours talking about it. He cried because he was so sad about losing his son, but he was just as upset about what happened to you. He knows what Dave used to do and I don't think he blames the whole thing on you at all. He is really a nice guy, Alex. He's not going to do anything to you, I promise."

"That's a giant relief, for sure," I said, thinking about how I'd just go from one jail smack dab into the middle of another one if that cop didn't know the whole story. I thought I shoulda been mad, but then I realized that Deonna had done me the biggest favor she ever could have by telling Dave's dad what happened. Otherwise, he might have thought it was all my fault.

"There's one more thing I've got to tell you, and then I've got to go warm up," Deonna said. I thought she was gonna cry and it took her a real long time to come out with it.

"I still want to be your best friend, even though after I tell you what I did, you might not feel the same way. You've had a rough time, and I know things are going to be better for you. But for a while your mom was really a mess because she thought you weren't going to make it, and she was really hurting for money. I couldn't help her out, but I remembered how you said you had $250 stashed in your bed that you saved up. I didn't know if sneaking into your house and picking up the stuff you asked me for was the right thing to do. I was really tempted after I left you that day when you first asked me to help you escape the rehab program. So I actually went over to your place to see if I could find a key under the doormat or somewhere obvious."

"You did? No kiddin'?" Wow, what a pal, I thought, but she wasn't through tellin' me the whole thing yet.

"What I thought I would do was get your stuff for you like you asked me to. But just as I put your mat down, your mom walked up and scared me half to death. That's when I knew I couldn't do it. She looked terrible, Alex. So I said I came to talk with her, and I wound up telling her everything. She had already figured out most of it anyway, believe me. But I still felt funny, so I...".

Deonna kinda looked like a puppy when it chewed up your shoe and was ready to be smacked with a newspaper.

"So you what?" I said, and smiled at her to make her finish the story.

"I'm sorry, but I took the money out of your room and gave it to her."

"Wow. That's too much, Deonna," I said. "What did she do? I mean, did she give it to the police or somethin'?"

"No. She cried and said she was going to pay her adult school tuition with it so she could find a job where she'd be home every night. Your mom's really something, Alex. She didn't care about anything except having you back home."

"Well, you're somethin' else, Deonna. How come I never thought of doin' somethin' decent and honest like puttin' my mom through night school?"

"Your mind was on something else, maybe," Deonna said, looking nervously behind her at the courts. "Look. I've got to get this over with. See you later."

I thought to myself, Deonna Johnson, if you can still hang around with me after the stuff I've pulled, then it's a miracle, man. I grabbed her arm. "Hey, champ. Let's just start fresh from right here, okay?"

"Okay!"

"Now get out there and cream those goobers good. I wanna see you make them eat green fuzz, Johnson, I mean it." She ran off smiling like her face was gonna fall off, I swear, and then I remembered one more thing.

"Hey Deonna, come back for a second," I yelled.

"Yeah?"

"Well, after you win this thing and get on the team, let's whoop it up and really celebrate, I mean do it up right!"

Deonna got a worried look on her face like I meant let's get down and do up a few lines. "I don't know, Alex. I'm not into being around you anymore if you're going to do that sort of thing again. Sorry."

I couldn't believe the way she was still thinkin', just like nothin' had ever changed. Well, I'd always be me and she'd always be her, but that wouldn't keep us apart. I started to laugh so loud that you could hear it all the way back out to the street. "Hey, Deonna. I wasn't talkin' about THAT kinda partyin'! I was talkin' about ice cream and cake!"

Do I need to tell ya that we ate a lot of junk that day? Nope. When it comes to chowin' down, Deonna is the kinda girl who would go for it even if you tied her hands behind her back. The neat thing is that we're kinda alike that way, which is okay by me, because best friends should have at least one thing in common, right?

Turn for DEONNA's side of the story...

Turn for ALEX's side of the story...

FLIPSIDE FICTION
Because There Are Always Two Sides to Every Story

Alex The Great
Deonna

by
Barbara S. Cole

THE ROSEN PUBLISHING GROUP, Inc.
NEW YORK

Published in 1989 by The Rosen Publishing Group, Inc.
29 East 21st Street, New York, NY 10010

First Edition

Manufactured in the United States of America

Library of Congress Cataloging-In-Publication Data

Cole, Barbara S.
   Alex the great./by Barbara S. Cole.—1st ed.
      p.   cm. —(Flipside fiction)
   Issued back-to-back/head to toe.
   Summary: Presents two viewpoints about teens
and drugs, one from a girl on drugs and one from a
friend who tries to help her.
   [1. Drug abuse—Fiction.]   I. Title.   II. Series.
PZ7.C673414A1   1988   [Fic]—dc19   88-37104
ISBN 0-8239-0941-7:$12.95

Manufactured in the United States of America

ALEX THE GREAT
DEONNA
Chapter One

Alex's room had this big picture window on the far wall.
There were white drapes with horses printed on them about
four inches apart. The horses kind of danced around when
the wind blew. Otherwise, the place wasn't much to look at.
A hospital was the last place I wanted to be on a perfect day
like that one. You couldn't see them from the green plastic
chair I sat on, but somewhere outside sparrows and mourning
doves were singing. When you mix their songs together, it
kind of sounds like one of those crackly opera stations on
the radio, only with birds instead of people. Maybe that's
what the birds were doing out there that day. I mean maybe
they were doing this whole opera for Alex. The sparrows
would be the happy ones, dittering on and on about how
great life is, and the mourning doves would come into the
scene every now and then with a funeral song.

Even though it was a nice hospital compared to the ones
I've been in, the only nice place to look was outside. A
couple of nurses were gaming at a table and there was lots of
grass, all clipped like it was fake or something. I stared out
at that grass as long as I could so I wouldn't have to look at

Alex lying there, all mucky-looking like she was made out of squishy yellow gum or something. No matter how long I looked at the bright green on the ground, that noise kept bugging me. I still can't get it out of my head. The machine next to Alex's bed was making this high-pitched blip-beep-beep noise. It was enough to make a person go really crazy. But that was just the kind of stuff that Alex loved to listen to. She would say that if you listened to the rhythm of something, even if it was a dirty sneaker banging against the inside of a washing machine, that kind of noise would open up your brain cells. Well, it sure didn't do that for my brain cells! I tried to make the beeping noises blend in with the bird opera, but it didn't work. Maybe when I was a little kid I could've made it work, but then when I was little I could lie on my bed and make snow fall around my chest of drawers if I stared at it long enough. Alex would say, "Well, whadda ya know, Johnson, let's build a snowman!" But when I told my mom that I couldn't find my socks because my bureau was buried in a snow drift, she said, "Of course it's not. What an imagination you have." After that, I could never make it snow again, hard as I tried.

I guess I liked Alex because she was the kind of girl who could watch a television set without even turning it on and laugh and cry like she was watching the best movie she had ever seen. Alex was real big on sounds. She liked to turn the stereo up and sit in front of one of the speakers with the front cover off so she could see the rounded part on the front of the speaker jiggle. She would say that the little round cones on the front of the speaker danced in time to the music. But I knew that they jiggled a lot because she had the music turned up so loud that they were ready to blow out. Now guess what's next to her head? A little speaker that goes blip-beep-beep. If she could only have heard it, she would have either danced to it or turned it up higher.

The nurse who came in to check on her said that sometimes

people who are in a coma can hear you and sometimes they can't. The nurse had eyebrows like a clown's. They were drawn in big reddish brown arches way up on her forehead. Under them, though, her eyes were real sad. She fluffed up Alex's pillow and checked the tube going into her arm.

She sighed and said, "Why do young people do this to themselves?" like she didn't want me to answer. Then she looked at me with her sad green eyes and said, "You know what happened to her, don't you?"

I nodded my head becasue when I tried to say yes, my eyes got all watery and my nose started to swell up and sting inside. Whenever I cry, which isn't too often, I'm a real gusher. I either bawl my head off or don't let myself start crying in the first place.

"You ever going to tell someone, like Mrs. Starky?" she asked.

Alex's mother had been there that morning, talking to Alex and crying at the same time. There were about ten wadded-up tissues on the floor. I didn't want to seem like I was interrupting anything when I first got there, so I stood in the doorway until it seemed okay to go in. I heard Alex's mom blow her nose and say, "I promise you, baby, I'll get another job in town. I'll be home more often. Please wake up. Please don't die on me."

How could I tell Alex's mom anything then? She wouldn't want to hear what I would have to say. And anyway, who was I to her? I only saw her some weekend mornings when she'd be all tired out and half asleep from one of her flights or else she'd be leaving for one. I knew that to her I was just another kid hanging around their apartment.

Mrs. Starky would never know that I watched Alex turn into this crazed luny, and if she did know she'd ask me that one question I still don't know if I can answer. Even thinking about it makes my scalp get all prickly.

While I was there, some nurses came in once in a while to

look at Alex or turn up the noise on the beeping machine so that they could hear it better out in the hall. The door to her room was open. They were pushing dead people up and down the hall, real fast. The whole place smelled like that junk you use in biology class to store your frogs in. They tell you not to sniff it or you'll pass out. Alex never took a biology class or she would have been sniffing at the jars the minute the teacher's back was turned.

Alex hardly ever went to school. She would say that school couldn't teach her the real lessons of the world. I never knew exactly what she meant, but I felt it would sound too dumb if I asked. While I was in school every day, working my brains off to get halfway-decent grades, Alex would be at home, lying on the floor with a speaker on either side of her head, blasting herself full of weird tunes like you wouldn't believe. Sometimes she'd say, "You're such a jock, you wouldn't know." That's what she thought about me. Just a dumb jock. And until just a little while ago I thought she was the smartest thing that ever walked on two legs. I wasn't the only one who used to think she was really something. At school, we'd be walking around the campus checking things out and more than one kid would say, "Hey, it's Alex the Great!" At first I thought maybe they called her that because they thought she was so cool. I didn't figure out the real reason they called her that until much later.

Alex didn't even know that the nurses were out there listening to her beeping. Or maybe when you go into a coma you stop beeping. All I know is that she couldn't tell that I had been there, sitting still until my legs fell asleep, in that nasty green plastic chair. Maybe her body felt like my legs. What's really gross to think about is that maybe she didn't even know if some part of her body had fallen asleep. I always wondered what would happen if your leg fell asleep and you didn't do anything about it. Like, does it die separate from your other leg? I never asked Alex something like

that, because knowing her, she'd make her leg go to sleep and then just let it keep going to find out the answer. Being in the hospital with her told me that at least that one time, keeping my thoughts to myself was a good thing. I knew that she would have let her leg go to sleep forever and maybe even have had to get it cut off, just so she would know the answer. That's how she was. And maybe when you're in a coma, that's how you are, sort of buzzing around numb. Your body probably feels like it's fake or something. Alex did look kind of fake. She didn't look any better than what was under those lumpy white sheets that were taking rides down the hallway.

I heard somewhere that they stick you in a refrigerator if you die in a hospital. They tie a wire tag around your toe like what they do in a hardware store when lawn mowers are on sale. They hang a big yellow paper tag with a model number on it from the handlebars of the mowers. That's all you get, which isn't much better than what a weed-eater gets. If they put the wrong tag on your toe, they don't know who you are until someone comes to look at you. Ever seen someone who's dead? It's gnarly. I saw a dead guy just last week. It was someone I knew, too. He died in Alex's car. Forget the blood. The blood was everywhere, even on Alex. Alex was one of the whitest white girls at our school. But when I saw her after the accident she was about the same color as the walls of her hospital room. Long blue veins showed through the skin of her arms. Sick. Isn't your blood still supposed to pump around and keep you pink if you're a white girl in a coma? What if she's really as good as dead or whatever stage you get to just before you're dead. And if she's lying there dead, is it my fault? I mean, I told her a million times, "Alex, you're crazy. You keep doing the works the way you are, and you'll wind up dead." But so what? Lot of good it did. I could have told her I'd rat on her and she could bet on it if she kept on like she was doing. But then, I'm supposed to be her friend. She never ratted on me. You just don't do

that, or at least I think you don't, when somebody you like is walking around with a head full of base. Well, maybe you do, I don't know. Even if she wound up hating me, at least she wouldn't have wound up hooked to that machine, stuck in the arm and up her nose with all those tubes and wires. Where does that stuff they pump into you go? Probably it's the same junk Alex did, just more legal. I can think of one time not too long ago when Alex wanted to rip off booze from a liquor store near our school. She played it cool for me when the time came, because she knew that if she didn't protect me my whole career could go down the tubes. How could I even think about letting someone know that she might be in trouble after she took care of me? I couldn't do it. Then I took another look at her and wondered for the zillionth time that day if maybe the rules don't count sometimes.

Once I tried to tell Alex that maybe all the junk she was sticking up her nose was the reason she felt so crummy all the time.

"Cocaine's been used by doctors since the beginning of time," she yelled. "Now get off my back, will ya?" So much for trying to tell Alex Starky what she should or shouldn't do!

What kind of sheets were those, anyway? I mean the ones they covered dead people with before they wheeled them down the hall?

I'm my parents' only kid, and I have my own single bed in our house. Our house isn't very big, but it gets to be a real pain when it's time to do chores unless you've got some kind of plan like I do. Let say it's my day to change the sheets. We have a guest bedroom, a room for my parents, and my room. First I change the sheets in my folks' room. They're king sized. When Aunt Martha can't deal with Uncle Raymond's getting drunk, she drops him off at our house to dry out. Unfortunately, she drops him off after midnight when it's a real hassle to be getting the guest bed ready for Uncle Ray. That's why I like to do all our rooms at the same time.

It used to be that Uncle Ray would only come over about every other month or so. But this last year he's had to stay with us twice or even three times in a month. His sheets have to be changed every day. On the first day he comes over he stinks like somebody had poured cigarette butts, trash-can juice (you know, the stuff that drips out from old vegetables and wet plastic bags into the bottom of the trash can and stinks like something died down there), and whiskey all over them. On the second day his sheets smell like tired old skin that's been soaking in vinegar. By the third day his sheets only smell like sweat a little. It's been this way for so long that I know this means he's dried out and Aunt Martha will come and pick him up.

Anyway, none of our sheets at home are the size of those sheets I saw outside of Alex's room on top of the dead bodies. I just wonder if the folks who make them know what's going to happen to them when they are taken out of the package. And then once they cover up someone who's croaked, do they bury it with the body? Or when they get rid of the body, do they send the sheet to the laundry and then somebody else gets it? Well, one thing's for sure. I could never be a nurse. Just thinking about using the same heating pad on another patient after I used it on one who died would give me the creeps. If this thing with Alex blows over, if she wakes up and never tells anyone about what really happened, I'll get on the varsity tennis team in the fall and it'll be like nothing ever happened. I'm sure not going to wind up being a nurse wheeling dead people around, painting giant eyebrows on myself, and having to do disgusting things like stick long plastic tubes up people's veins!

Once Mom said that I should learn a skill that I could fall back on. You know, something you could do that people would always need, like typing or cutting hair. I think she even said something about going to nursing school. Well, I don't care if nurses make good money, and I don't care about

getting a dumb steady paycheck. I want to be on the front of one of those cereal boxes. Breakfast of champions. And me *me* ME starring as the champion. Besides, you could make millions. Then I could have all the fancy clothes I want, and have new ones made just for me. Not like some of the stuff Alex has worn. Those were trash. Well, let's say they don't look like trash the way she wears them. She's so skinny, anything would look great on her. Or at least it did. I keep forgetting she's laid up in that bed. She didn't open her eyes. She was barely breathing.

One time when I just dropped in on Alex, the front door was open a little and so I just went in, because I heard a funny noise. There she was on the floor with her head between the stereo speakers. Her mouth was open a little and the noise turned out to be really gnarly snoring. It's amazing that nobody in her building even complained about the noises coming from that living room.

Nothing about Alex was quiet. She wore all kinds of crazy stuff, like rags from old faded towels that she'd braid into her hair. On a sunny day you could see her coming a mile away because she had zippers and sequins all over her T-shirt and pants. Then there was always her flaming hair flying all over the place. Sometime she'd tease it and use tons of her mom's hairspray so it would stick straight out in the back. It looked more like orangy spaghetti that hadn't been cooked. And she's covered with freckles, but I didn't really notice them in the hospital. I guess when you're in a coma, your freckles fade. Even her hair wasn't as brassy-looking as it used to be. The nurses must have either cut most of it away or tucked it into her gown because all you could see was this pale little face with no life in it, like a ghost's face. She matched the nurses' uniforms. Maybe she was even whiter than that. It was so weird to see her quiet like that.

Chapter Two

It's just strange right now. It's like I'm not sure about anything. I don't know if I'll ever make the team after all the trouble I've gotten into this last semester, and I don't even know if someone I thought was my friend is alive or dead. If she's dead, it's probably my fault because I didn't stop her, I didn't tell her mom or my folks. I'm afraid if she dies I'll never have anybody to talk to again, but if she doesn't I could wind up with no future. Of course everybody will ask her what happened. That means no practice, no tournaments, no clinics, no lessons, no coaching. It also means I could wind up being a nurse. Now what kind of exercise can you get being a nurse?

Already, my arms are shrinking. My bones ache because they want to run the track every day like I used to. I wake up in the middle of the night and I can't sleep because I want to play hard, I want to sweat a lot, and you can't work up a sweat taking out the trash.

Sometimes when I can't sleep I go into the kitchen and stand on the cold tiles. The cold makes my bones ache worse than they ached when I was in bed, trying not to squirm around. Everything in me wants to squirm around. Sometimes it's my arms, sometimes it's my head. But lately it's just my legs. My legs want to move, I mean really move, like

11

just fly for a while. You get used to them being pumped up with blood. If Alex wakes up and tells anyone what really happened, my legs will be screaming in pain, throwing all kinds of fits to punish me for not letting them loose every day like they're used to. My parents will never trust anything I say for the rest of my life. They wouldn't even know how painful it would be for me to be in my room all the time. Mom would say, "You should put your mind more on your studies, dear." Or she'd say, "Go stand on the bathroom floor. When I had growing pains, that is what your Grandma Bell used to say. And it did work."

Maybe I could do more chores to get rid of the aching I would feel if they put me on restriction because they found out what happened. I would wash cars and paint the house, but even that wouldn't be good enough. I'd be shrinking right before my very eyes.

Mom would think I was just developing a better figure than before my punishment. She'd think I was slimmer, but it would be my body shucking off all that hard-earned power. Mom wasn't an athlete when she was my age. She was just like all the other girls in her school—chasing after boys like she had come down with some disease of the mind. That's how it is at my school, too. Mom doesn't like it that I have the body of an athlete. She doesn't have a clue about how good it feels. I don't even try to tell her anymore. Once, when I did, I said, "When you're really healthy, I mean so healthy that your skin tingles, the blood feels like it whooshes all the way from your head to your toes. You're always warm. You want to leap like a cat! You feel like there's nothing you can't do. That's how good it feels to have a body like mine."

"That's very nice. But it just doesn't look, well, you know, feminine. You aren't supposed to have muscles around your knee caps, and look at the big veins on the sides of your calves. I'm worried about you, you know. You should have

begun menstruating by now. You should be a little more, well, developed. Don't you want to be like the rest of the sophomore girls?"

"Forget it. I've got better things to do than smear crud all over my face and talk like an idiot about those tiny little bugs that everyone calls 'boys'. And who needs boobs? They just get in the way."

"Deonna! You're bound to get breasts sometime, and when you do, I hope you'll accept and appreciate them. There's nothing wrong with being a woman."

"I know that, except if being a woman means acting stupid and feeling like trash, I'd rather be dead."

"That's enough," Mom said, scowling at me. I always know not to push her when she gets that deep long crease between her eyebrows. It means more trouble's coming. Nobody, not even Dad, pushes Mom past that point!

Even if nobody at school likes me, I know they like my body. Maybe it isn't like the other girls', but then how come I can feel everybody's eyes on me even when my back is turned? I can hear the Chicano girls whispering real fast in Spanish. I don't know any Spanish, but I know they're talking about my biceps and wishing they were as tight as me. Some of those girls pick off the black girls after school or at lunch and try to beat them up. The black girls walk in groups or get rides home. But not me. No Chicano girl ever once tried to pick on me, because I've got veins in my hands and muscles in my forearms, especially my right one from playing tennis all the time. They know I could smash them flat into the ground.

Mom says, "Nothing is worse than a young girl with big biceps. It's not as God intended, just remember that." Well, Mom went to an all-black Catholic school. She never had to do what I'm doing. All she wanted to do was get married, just like all the other girls she went to school with. So as far as Mom's opinion goes, forget it. Mom is telling me what

God wants. She says that God wants me to have a skinny little body like Alex's body. But Mom hates Alex, and she hates Alex's mother, too. She wants me to look like her, but not act like her. Sometimes when she's acting so high and mighty, I'd give up my best pair of sneakers to be able to tell her the truth about Alex. Or at least let her know how you really get a skinny little body like that.

If you're like Alex, here's how you stay skinny. You sneak out of the house every night, climb into some guy's car you don't even know, let him get you into one of the clubs with a fake i.d., snort coke, drink beer, and dance until you're so sick you don't know what's what anymore. Then if you're lucky you get a ride home. Otherwise, you walk all the way. That gets you pretty skinny. But by then it's just about dawn and you have to sneak back into your house all drunk and hyped and everything else and lie there on your bed trying not to puke, because if you do your mom will wake up and when she goes to get you soda crackers and fizzy water, she'll see how wrecked out you are and wham, you're not only sick as a dog, you're in real big trouble. That's how Alex stayed skinny. I wish I could tell Mom that, maybe not just to let her know I'm no dummy, but to let her know at least part of what really happened. I feel like I'm carrying around a sack of cement because I can't say anything.

Alex said she liked to have a good time, all the time.

"Life's too short, Deonna. You can waste yours sweating like a pig and rubbing goop into your muscles when you pull 'em and twist 'em like rubber bands, but not me. That's not how I like to do it. To be great, you gotta experience tons of things."

Well, that IS how I like to do it, and I don't see that she's having such a great time where she's at right now. At least I'm alive.

Guess I'm mad because I'm stuck. I would have been able to call Alex on the phone just to talk and maybe try to figure

things out, but now who can I talk to? Alex and me, we were pretty close these last couple of years. When I was a freshman, I thought I was going to run away from home just to keep from having to face school every day. My old school was a place where everybody was friends and pretty much all alike, and Edison is this giant school where everybody is all mixed up together. If you saw how they all clumped up into groups even on the first day of orientation, you'd know there was going to be trouble. It didn't make any sense to Alex and me. But Alex always knew what to do, and she got in tight with everybody. I was stuck, same as I am now. I had to hang out with her or else be by myself, which wasn't a good thing to do, especially then.

Now it's probably going to be like it used to be. Just classes and classes and classes, no people, and no fun. Either way you look at it, this whole thing stinks.

Chapter Three

Last night someone was banging and yelling like crazy outside our front door. It was about midnight and we were all in bed. I was having a lot of trouble going to sleep. I was the first one up. I wondered whether I should go to the door. What if it was somebody with a gun? That sort of thing is supposed to happen all the time. Maybe there was a fight going on outside. No matter how scared I was, I had to see what was going on. I knocked on my parents' door. I heard my mother mumble something right in the middle of a long, nasty-sounding snore. Whoever was banging on the door was doing it hard enough to break it down.

"Mal, go see who it is," Mom said behind the door.

"Go back to sleep, it's nothing", he said.

"MALCOLM!"

I heard the banging of Dad's feet on the floor. "I'm getting tired of this. You know it's only Ray."

Mom was wide awake now. "Again? He was here just last week." She sounded pretty mad.

"Martha said he's been at it again since yesterday morning. Let him sit for a while."

"I need my sleep, too, you know! And what about the neighbors? Besides, it's freezing cold out there and he could get pneumonia."

As soon as I heard the thumping of Dad's feet getting near their bedroom door, I ran into the living room to see who was outside. Usually, if it was Uncle Ray, Aunt Martha would just drop him off on the doorstep and scream at him from the car. I never got to see him until the next day, after Mom had made him shower and shave and have something to eat.

Dad looked through the peephole and then cussed as he undid the locks on the front door. The little half circle of hair on the back of his head was all flattened down.

"Get in here, Ray, what you trying to do, wake up the neighborhood?" Dad was looking down at the two steps that led to our front door. I crept up behind him to get a better view.

"Can't get up, man. I got it stuck. It got stuck and I couldn't pull it down..." Sitting on the bottom step was Uncle Ray, mumbling into his big hands as he hid his face from Dad. I stepped out into the doorway to get a better look. Dad looked down at me like he was going to swat me, but then the angry look went out of his eyes and he said in a soft voice, "Deonna, go get a towel, then you get back to bed. I don't want you to see this."

"But I want to," I said, not wanting to leave.

"Get that rug rat out of here. Don't wanner to see her Unca Ray like this." Uncle Raymond wouldn't get up, even though Dad was leaning over to help him to his feet.

"Get me a towel now!" Dad shouted at me.

When I found a towel that was wrecked enough so we could throw it away after Uncle Ray used it, I brought it back into the living room. Dad was blocking the door with his body. He's so big that I could barely see past him to where Uncle Ray was still sitting.

"Close your eyes, throw me the towel, and then get back to bed."

But too late, I saw it all. Uncle Ray had caught his zipper

in the material of his fly and had to pee all over himself. Then I guess he got sick and barfed everywhere. He stank so bad!

If he didn't want me to see him that way, why show up here at all? Why not just spend the night out by some giant dumpster like all the other drunks do? Where was Aunt Martha this time? Usually she would drop him off and scream at him for a while.

Dad was mumbling to himself as he marched Uncle Ray down the hall to the bathroom.

"Ray, Ray, Ray. What the sam hill goes on in that brain of yours that makes you do this to yourself? Don't you know you are a Johnson? Where's your pride, man?" Dad closed the bathroom door, but I could still hear his low grumbling voice from behind the door.

"Martha kicked me out. Said, 'You gonna act like a bum, then get out and be a real one,' So what'sa man supposed to do. Tell me. But then, it got stuck..."

"You're a mess. You stink like something else, man," I heard Dad say.

"I'm gonna be sick again, Malcolm. Real sick...". Then I heard Uncle Ray heaving. How could Dad stand being in there with him, with that stink and the rotten clothes and the retching noises Uncle Ray was making? I'm one of those types, you know, who can't stand to hear the sound of somebody barfing. If I can't get away fast enough I start gagging myself. That's what happened. I closed my bedroom door, but it was too late. I went to my window and slid it wide open. There was nothing out there but the usual brick wall lined with trash cans. They were full of old lawn mower clippings and yesterday's garbage. I wanted to stick my whole head out the window, but there were those ugly black bars over them. When we first moved into this house, I thought my parents put them on the windows on purpose to keep me inside all the time. But they were there before. If

there's a fire, we are supposed to go out the front way. The front windows have these safety locks on them. Dad says that somebody would have to break glass to get inside. We have insurance so that if we aren't home, we could get back everything that was stolen, but he says that if we are home and somebody breaks the glass, that would give him enough time to load up his pistol. But nothing like that ever happens in this neighborhood. The biggest thing that ever happens around here is Uncle Ray and Aunt Martha making a fuss outside the house. So far, nobody has complained to us about it.

Since I couldn't hear Uncle Ray throwing up any more, I felt better. It was foggy outside, and the cold wet air woke me up all the way and made me feel like jabbering. So I flopped on my bed and called Alex's number. I knew if I talked real quiet, my parents wouldn't know I was on the phone. Alex's mom was away on a bunch of flights, so I knew I wouldn't wake her up.

"Yeah? Whadda ya want?" Alex sounded like she was completely awake.

"It's just me. You got a minute?"

"It's a drag tonight, there's nothin' happening. You might as well talk your head off. I'm so bored, I did a little crystal, and I was savin' that up for a real party. Stuff's hard to come by these days, after they busted the house next door to the school. What's up?"

"My Uncle Ray's at it again," I said.

"The drunk guy? Maybe he needs something to put him down for a while. I could look around here, I've got everything tonight. Stocked totally." I could hear rattling noises like bottles being shaken on Alex's end of the phone.

"No. You'd kill him. He's really sick. He drank too much after my aunt threw him out. Now he's upchucking all over the place."

"Well, that's life, kiddo. You do the crime, you do the

time. Part of the whoopee and all that."

"Yeah, but does he have to wake up the whole neighborhood? I have to get my sleep or else tomorrow's practice is a real washout."

"You know, Johnson, you're a real prude. Now there's your only uncle in the world feelin' pretty bad, and your dad has to go to work at some hairy bomb factory every day, and you're worrying about your jog around the track."

"I am not! But you'd get sick of it if your mom did this all the time like Ray does," I said.

Alex snorted, "Hah! My mother snitches little Stoli bottles from the plane and gives them away. I mean, the little ones you have tea parties with when you're a kid. I get all the ones she doesn't take from her bag before she unpacks. She never drinks them, can you believe it? She's got a gold mine in her bag and she doesn't want any of it. She says she puts on too much weight just breathing, much less drinking."

"So that's what's clanking in your book bag every morning?"

"Wouldn't you like to know, nosy!" Alex laughed.

"Then why is your bag so heavy in the morning? You don't carry books, that's for sure."

"It's just stuff, that's all. Nothing you'd be interested in," Alex said.

"How would you know? Maybe sometime..."

"Johnson, the day you loosen up and party, even a little, is the day I drop dead. Just forget it. You're not the type, everybody knows that by now. Deonna Johnson does not like to party," she said, making fun of me.

"You should see my Uncle Ray. He doesn't look like he's been to any parties lately."

"You just don't know about life, Johnson. Someday somebody's gonna have to make you wise up. Like right now, for instance."

"For instance what?"

"I mean, here I am, all by myself, nobody's home in this stinkin' little box, and I'm having a wingding all by myself. No help, no friends."

"How do you do that?" I asked.

"First, you put on some great music. Something kind of eerie that has lots of echoey stuff in it. Like a jazz station. It gets you in the right mood. Then you get the speakers set just right, one on each side of your head so you can hear everything."

"So? What's so big about that?"

"Don't you know anything? It opens up your brain cells. Prepares 'em. Puts you in the mood for some heavy activity. But then comes the really fun part, and you can't do this when you have lots of friends over, because they'll get bored fast. But just me, well, I have a great time."

"What's that?" I asked.

"Well, then you make yourself a real stiff drink, for starters."

"What kind of drink?"

"I swear, Johnson," Alex sighed with impatience, "you make a really strong one, like whiskey straight up. See, what it does is relax your muscles and fix you up good. Then you switch the station on the radio to something that has a steady beat. Like thump-thump-thumpy stuff. Dance music, if you can find it. Then, before you really get relaxed, you do up a few lines. Like three, for instance, but you only do the next one just when the last one starts to let you down a little bit."

"Don't you get sick or tired or anything?" I could hear my uncle throw up again in the background while I listened to Alex talk.

"That's only for old farts like your uncle. Me, I like to dance. Like right now!" The phone crashed onto something hard at Alex's end, and I could hear her screaming in the background, "Like this, Johnson!" Then the stereo was blasting drum beats and I could hear these guys singing

words like, "You gotta get down, get down, GET WAY DOWN," over and over again.

"What the hell are you doing up, young lady?" It was Mom, sticking her head into my room. Her eyes were sleepy, but she looked angry.

"Just talking on the phone," I said.

"To that sleazy friend of yours, Ignatz? You get off the phone this minute and get your butt into that bed. Now!"

"Her name is not Ignatz. It's Alex."

"I don't care if her name is Rumpelstiltskin! You heard me, cut if off now!" Then she slammed the door so hard that a poster fell off the wall. It ripped when it hit the carpet. My favorite one, with the woman's body cut in half showing all the veins, muscles, and bones.

"Alex, Alex—I gotta go. Alex." But she was not anywhere near the phone. All I could hear was stomping noises and those voices from the stereo saying, "That's right, do it tonight. Get down, get down. Get way way down down."

It was quiet in the house. Dad must have put Uncle Ray to bed. I turned off the lights and crawled back into bed. It was 1:45 in the morning. I reset my alarm clock so I could sleep an extra half hour. I knew I'd feel lousy the next day. When I try to work out without enough sleep, it feels like somebody took a box of oatmeal and stuffed it into my head and tied soup cans to my arms and legs. I switched off the lamp next to the telephone and thought about Alex. I knew she'd be up all night long, jumping on the couch and tossing her long red hair all over her head like it was a whip. But I felt funny hanging up on her. What if she got sick like Uncle Ray and nobody was around to help her out? What if somebody in her apartment building complained to the police and they found out that Alex's mother is hardly ever at home? What if she fainted and there was a fire? How come she doesn't worry about this kind of stuff happening?

I tried to think of nicer things so I could fall asleep, but

nothing came to me except the way Uncle Raymond's pants looked and the crud all over his shirt. His eyes were like big black holes and there was nothing inside when you looked at them. Why does he do it? What makes him want to be that way? Especially if it makes him sick as a dog. I started thinking about him throwing up and felt sick myself again. My head hurt. When I think too much, I get a headache. I tried lying on my side so it would hurt in a different spot for a while. Every time the blood pounded in my head, I heard the thump of Alex's music. Everybody listens to that kind of music now. What does it really mean, "get down, get down, get way down"? I must be missing something. Maybe I'm just a prude. What do they know that I don't know? They must know something, or else why would they do what they do to themselves? Is it really that much fun that it's worth barfing over?

Chapter Four

It's still weird to think of her not calling me up and asking me to drop by just to do nothing. I liked doing nothing with Alex. Somehow we'd start out to do nothing, and by the time I was ready to leave we'd have repainted her bedroom, or baked so many cookies that we could've given cavities to our entire school. That's a lot of kids. We go to the biggest school in San Francisco. Last June we had to take over part of Candlestick Park because the graduating class was so big that there was nowhere to put everybody on the campus.

Alex was about the only white girl at school that I liked. Once I even got up the guts to tell her that. She said, "Yeah? And you're the only black girl in this stinkin' jail I like, too. 'Cept you're probably the only black girl in the place, period." Well, that couldn't have been true because there's lots of black kids at Edison High.

I don't think there's a school anywhere with as many different kinds of people in it. It causes lots of problems all the time, even though it's really just a bunch of small things, not anything that would get on the front of the newspaper. Usually it just gets kind of uncomfortable. After school you can walk around and see five fights going on at the same time. Even the parking lot is divided up. The low-riders hang out closest to the street, and when the blacks try to

drive home the Chicanos pull their big cars across the driveway and block it so nobody can get out. The white guys have the section near the playing field. When the Chinese guys hassle them, they just drive out to the street by tearing out over the yard. But this school is supposed to be a good example of how we can all get it together. Alex and I used to laugh a lot about what a joke that was.

One time I went into the bathroom in the English hall and there were about five low-rider girls hanging out smoking dope and talking. As soon as I saw them I tried to turn around and go out the swinging door to get away from them. But this one girl with a black fish net blouse and lots of pink eye makeup stood in front of the door.

"Is this the snitch, Maria? 'Cause if she's the one, she's dead, man."

Another girl with hair like a giant ant hill said, "Nah. That one is a white girl. This one's friends with Alex the Great. You know, that white chick with the good stuff? She's cool."

A bony girl with jet black hair that had a purple stripe in it came out of one of the stalls wiping her nose and sniffing a lot.

"You tell me, chickie-girl," she said with a thick accent, "what's this Alex the Great to you?"

"Yeah, what's so damn great that you hang out with her, anyway?" asked another girl with crater marks on her face and a purple stripe in her hair like the other one.

I didn't know what stuff they meant. I was afraid there were too many of them and they wouldn't let me out. I know there's times you should be softer, but I thought maybe if these girls saw a really insane black girl with muscles, they wouldn't know what to do but lay off. So I walked right up to the leader who was wiping her nose, got up real close to her face and squinted my eyes. I stared at her for a few seconds, and she looked at me like she was getting scared.

Just as Alex would do in a situation like that, I said, "Go

ask her yourself, ya hear?" Then I shoved past the other girls and walked out into the hall feeling pretty good.

No matter what has happened to me these past few months because of her, I still feel the same way about Alex, even though I should be totally mad about what she made me do and how it all turned out.

I still feel she's my best friend even though sometimes I think I would have been better off if we had never hung out together. If it weren't for her, I wouldn't be sitting here on my bed getting fat instead of working out. I feel like opening the window and screaming out at the trash cans, but I'm not the type who make scenes. My folks would think I was on dope.

One time, Mom had me get up on an old stepladder to change a light bulb in the kitchen ceiling. I'm a little scared of heights, so climbing up on something that was wobbling, plus looking down at the top of Mom's gray hair from an angle I never saw before was a real feat. Dad was working late, and nobody else was around who was tall enough to change the bulb before it got dark outside. The ladder wasn't tall enough to get me all the way to the top of the fixture so I could unscrew it and put in a new bulb, so I had to stand on tiptoe and hold my arm up so high above my head that I felt the socket in my shoulder pull apart. I couldn't look up, or I'd lose some of the reach I had, so I put my head down and kept stretching to untwist the screws holding the fixture to the ceiling. But just before that, I had been practicing volleys with the automatic ball machine, and my strong arm was like jelly. I kept having to put my arm down and shake it to get the blood back into it. Just as I was getting to the last screw, Mom yelled, "Get down here and let me see your eyeballs!"

"What?" I said, because I could hardly believe how weird she sounded.

"Get down here, Deonna. Open up your eyes. Wide. Face

the kitchen window. Why are your pupils so dilated?"

"I don't know. What are you getting all freaked out about?" I said.

"I know it like I know there's a God in heaven. You're messing around with drugs. That's why you can't hold your arm up long enough to get that fixture down." Mom's voice was loud and wobbly all at the same time. Even though the light was not so good anymore, I could see how mad she was by the way her laugh lines bunched up together. When she's happy, they go from the corners of her eyes down to her earlobes. But if she gets mad, they squish up and look like a cat's whiskers that mothers draw on their kids' faces at Halloween.

"Mom, I don't do that, and you know it. It's dark in here, that's why my eyes are funny. And I played tennis real hard just before I came home. So that's why my arm..."

"I've read the newspaper. I've seen television and I know what's going on in this world," Mom said, and she grabbed my chin with her hand. It felt sweaty, but she still had a good grip on my face and she shook it a little. "Don't think you can get away with it. I'm watching you every minute. I don't like what you kids do in school. I don't like your friends, and I don't like it when I see my own daughter unable to screw in a light bulb."

"Well, I could if I could reach it," I yelled, but I knew by the look on her face that nothing I said would do any good, so I just let her shake my jaw and get it over with.

"You want to wind up like your Uncle Raymond? Or like your Grandpa Bell? Good for nothing? Go right ahead. But do it out in the street. And don't come running to me when you're hungry or so sick you can't walk anymore. You want that kind of life, then just keep it up, young lady. I mean it. You just keep it right up."

Man! If I could have supported myself, I would have run out the door and not come back. She didn't know how bad it

hurt when she talked to me like that. But I can't run away. I'm counting on being a tennis star. I don't know how to do anything but yard work and house cleaning, and I'll be damned if I'm going to wind up being a nurse. So I had to stay put and take it. But it made me think: She's accusing me of doing something I try real hard every day not to do. She thinks I already get loaded. And I never even did it once! I don't know what it feels like. Why did she do that to me?

Alex's mom is nothing like my mom. Well, I mean besides being kind of young and pretty. Alex sort of looks like her mom, but if you tell her that she'll hate you forever because she thinks her mom is a corn ball. She calls her "The Fluff" when she's not around, which is most of the time. Alex's mom is cool. Whenever she's not flying off somewhere neat, like Japan, she's home just relaxing. She has jet lag all the time. I've never been anywhere except just outside San Francisco, so I wouldn't even know how it feels to wake up in another city every day. But someday maybe I'll get to go wherever I want. Like to Wimbledon or Australia.

Sometimes I would go over to see Alex and her mom would be there, singing in the bathroom.

"Who's that?" I asked, the first time I went to their small apartment.

"It's The Fluff again. Doin' her nails, gettin' herself all done up like a poodle in heat. Except you know what?" Alex slapped her leg like she had a good punch line ready. "She isn't going anywhere! The Fluff gets all done up when she comes home, but when she goes around the world twice a month she doesn't wear anything more than rouge and lipstick. What a crack-up, I swear!"

"Huh," I said, not really knowing what to say. How do you talk about your parents like that? I never did in front of anyone, even though I might have thought like Alex did, sort of.

My parents are more conservative than Alex's mom. They take one look at people and figure out whether they can trust

them or not. That's what they did when they first met Alex. She and I met in the gym during physical education, because that was the last class of the day for both of us. Alex wasn't wearing the green shorts with the yellow stripes and the white cotton T-shirt like everybody else was wearing. She stuck out of the crowd like a sore thumb. Everybody took this slow stretch class because it sounded like the easiest way to get out of doing anything really sweaty. I took it because I really wanted to stretch.

Anyway, in class Alex came over and asked if I'd show her how I got my knees to stretch all the way down to the floor when we were trying to loosen up our inner thigh muscles. I showed her, but then instead of doing the exercise, she talked up a blue streak for the rest of the class. I was afraid we'd get caught, but since we were all the way in the back of the gym, the teacher couldn't hear or see us. After that, we dressed and walked out of the locker room toward the main part of the school. I hadn't had a chance to say very much because Alex was doing all the talking like she usually did, but when I did get in a few words I asked her if she'd like to come over to my house.

Her place was on the way from school, so she said we could walk together. Then we went into my house. Dad was home early because he had a headache. He was lying on the couch with a washrag over his eyes. Mom was sitting at the end of the couch rubbing his feet and watching the news on TV. Everything was fine until Alex walked into the room behind me. The way they looked at her, you'd think I'd brought in a dinosaur or an elephant. They just stared. She was one of the first kids from school that ever came home with me, and I thought maybe they were surprised because I picked a white girl. I said, "This is Alex Starky from school." But neither of them said anything. It was so weird that I showed Alex through the house and then told her I had better get to my homework before dinner. She didn't seem to think anything was strange about how my parents were acting and just said

she'd see me the next day.

"Who was that?" Dad asked, when I came back after walking Alex part of the way down the street.

"Or rather, WHAT was that?" said Mom.

"Is that what the kids look like at school nowadays? My God, things've really changed." Dad sat up on the couch, holding the rag against his head again.

"What's wrong? She's a nice girl. If you think SHE's weird-looking, you should see some of the other girls at school. That's nothing," I said, but I could see that they couldn't care less what I thought.

With one look, all they thought about her is that she's the kind of girl I shouldn't be hanging around with. But they didn't know her like I did. Alex was more than just a hubba freak, more than a chick who wore crazy clothes. At least she was to me. It's like everyone at school knew her for something different. The guys liked her because she was sort of a tossup, I guess. Sometimes she couldn't get up enough money for her own works, so she'd get real friendly with them and then ask them for favors. They'd lend her money all the time. The girls treated her like she was a star sometimes. Either they'd talk about her behind her back or try to hang out with her and copy the way she dressed. But Alex said they were all clones and she wouldn't have much to do with any of them. I wondered why she hung out with me all the time, but when I asked her, all of a sudden she'd get kind of embarrassed and say, "Because you're different."

Alex had lots of guys who were her friends. I thought they were strange, but the stranger they were, the more Alex seemed to like them.

"Deonna," Alex said when I asked her how come she liked to hang around with guys that looked like they hadn't taken a shower for weeks, "you gotta stop lookin' at the outsides of people, ya know what I mean? It's like there's this guy, Rabbit. He can't barely speak, he hates being around people,

but if ya got to know him you'd find out that he has this great singing voice and he knows all the words to every Joni Mitchell song. Every one!"

"Who's Joni Mitchell?" I asked.

"Come over some afternoon and Rabitt'll bring every single thing she's ever done. The words are on the back. Nobody knows about her. They think she's kind of a hippie has-been, but that's not how it is."

"So?"

"So if you look at Rabbit's ugly face, his giant ears that stick out of that stringy, greasy head of his, and see how his teeth jut out of his lips, you'd never get the chance to know what he knows about music. See what I'm gettin' at?"

You'd think that someone like Alex would think as well about herself as she thought about other people. But I've seen her do things to herself that just don't line up with what she tried to make me think.

Like one time, I told Alex that she ought to get herself into shape.

"I'm no jock like you, Johnson. I'm a member of the loose flesh team."

"Yeah, but you'll feel good. Don't you ever want to wake up and kind of spring out of bed in the morning?"

"If I want to spring out of bed, I make sure I never get into it in the first place," Alex said.

"It's easy if you're buzzed out, that's for sure. No. What I mean is, don't you ever want to feel good, all by yourself without getting freaked on coke first?"

"You're startin' to sound like one of those commercials. You know, the one where they show you a thirty-second shot of an egg frying in a greasy pan and tell you that's your brain on drugs? Do I look bad? Do I act retarded? Then how do you figure that's the truth?"

"Nobody's arguing with you. I just thought you might like to get into something more natural, is all."

Talking to Alex was like talking to a wall unless you were saying something she wanted to hear. I know I thought she was smarter than me, but nothing is worse than knowing you are right and arguing with someone who can make you feel like you're dumb and wrong at the same time.

Anyway, Alex showed up to the the one-mile walk and run test with highbeams the size of pizzas. You could see them even behind those pink cat-eye sunglasses with the rhinestones in each corner.

"I'm gonna show you that I'm in great shape, Johnson. I'm gonna beat everybody's time in the entire school. If this were a real race, not some fuddy-duddy political thing like it is, I'd get a gold medal. You watch."

I tried to tell her not to do it, but what could I say to change her mind? You don't change Alex's mind. You wait until it wears out first. We started off running together, picking up one Popsicle stick each time we ran around the track. Then all of a sudden Alex said, "See ya, slow poke," and took off like she had rocket fuel for lunch. She ran around the track two times to my one, making funny faces at the teacher and some of the girls who had already dropped out.

"I'm gonna do it again, Johnson, until you admit that I'm in the greatest shape ever. I'm Alex the Great no matter what I eat, snort, or smoke." Then she ran around the track again, stopping next to me to try and get me to admit she was great. But I couldn't. I was running slowly to make it all the way to the five-minute mark without having to walk. Meanwhile, I was worried about her running like that. Nobody does that and lives! Just as I thought maybe I better tell her she was great no matter what, she stopped running and stood still at the part of the track that was farthest from the starting point. I started to run toward her, but before I could get there she stumbled from one side to the next and then fell straight back on the dirt. A second after I got to her, the teacher was down on the ground, listening to her heart. Some girl stand-

ing behind the teacher said, "Is she dead?" The teacher said, "No, she just fainted," and patted her face. Alex opened her eyes, looked up at me standing over her, and started laughing like she was out of her mind. The teacher walked away, looking really angry at Alex for fooling everybody.

"Say it, Deonna, just like everybody else says it." Alex got up and punched my arm and just kept laughing. I was so mad, I didn't want to talk to her. She made me think she was dead! "Go on," she said, "say, hey, it's Alex the Great."

"You're crazy, that's what you are," I said, then started to run back to where the teacher was standing to figure out what we were supposed to be doing next. Alex ran in the opposite direction, yelling all the way until I could barely hear her from the other side of the running field.

"You'll see, Johnson. It's true. I'm great no matter what. You say it or I'll prove it, even if I have to die trying. EVEN IF I HAVE TO DIE TRYING, JOHNSON," she screamed before she ran out of the field completely, "YOU HEAR ME?"

The teacher took off her sunglasses and blew her whistle to call everyone in from the field where they were doing other fitness tests. While everybody was running in, she said, "What's with Starky? Is she on something?"

I didn't say anything. I just shrugged and made a face that said I didn't know what her problem was.

"I feel really sorry for that kid. You better keep your eye on her. I think she's in for some big trouble if she doesn't straighten up," the teacher said. "But you're different, Deonna. Don't get mixed up with kids like that. You've still got a chance."

Well, that made me mad. Who is this P.E. teacher to tell me who to hang out with and who not to? Where was she when her friends needed her? I bet if she came around the block one day after school and saw all these Chicano girls beating up on one of her friends, she would have just kept

on going. But that's not how I am. When it happened just like that to Alex, I jumped right in and tried to help her out, even though she had some kind of problem way back then. Not everybody is made perfect right from the start. Not even that P.E. teacher.

"Alex has a chance, too," was all I said, but the teacher looked at me and shook her head like there was no hope. I thought I was right and she was wrong. Didn't Alex just beat out everybody, two to one? So maybe Alex is a little nutso. But I thought to myself, what's so wrong with being a little bit different, anyway? Then when I was changing in the locker room, I had a funny feeling inside. What if Alex really had passed out and just pretended that she was okay? What if she was sick?

Chapter Five

I went to Alex's locker with her. I think it was a Friday
because the next day there was supposed to be a big party.
She asked me to go to the party a long time ago, but it didn't
sound like too much fun at the time. I didn't know any of her
friends, and I didn't have anyone to go with who would get
along with Alex's kind of people. But she said that the party
was going to be at her place. Her mom was gone the entire
weekend, and Alex thought that she could clean up whatever mess there was and her mom would never know she had
anybody over. At her locker, she was trying to figure out the
combination of the lock because she always had trouble remembering it, and was talking about how she would get all
the things she needed.

"You going to help me this time?" Alex asked.

"I don't know. What do you need?"

"About three bottles of really hot stuff. This gig has got
to be fully kegged, ya know." She got her locker open and
tossed her heavy book bag in. It sounded like something
made of glass broke when the bag hit bottom.

"What's in there?" I asked.

"Everything but the kitchen sink, kiddo. This party is
going to be a real blow-out show, ya know? I've got everything stashed in here. 'Ludes, pink hearts, dynamite weed,

a little dust, and of course," she patted the bag so it lay flatter against the back of the locker, "lots of flake, more than you've even seen." Alex seemed so proud of herself.

"Promise you won't laugh?"

"Yeah, yeah, what is it?" said Alex, slamming shut the locker and twisting the dial on the lock.

"I've never seen flake. I don't even know what it is." I felt pretty dumb saying that to an expert like her.

"Are you kidding me, Deonna? I knew you didn't like to party, but I figured all you jock types did a little snort before every game. I mean, how do the pros win games, anyway?"

"They just practice, I guess. That's all I've been doing," I said.

"Amazing. Really amazing. I'm hanging around with a friggin' virgin who doesn't know what flake is! You're really something, you know? I've never in my life known anyone as untouched as you. Deonna, everybody in the whole world does something. Except you. Just forget about my party. You'd hate it."

"But what's so great about this flake stuff?" Alex walked away from me, flipping strands of hair off her shoulders. She didn't even turn around. I thought maybe I said something to make her mad, but I couldn't figure out what it was.

"Like I said, kiddo, just forget it. Stay as sweet as ya are and all that." Then Alex turned the corner and disappeared from the rows and rows of army green lockers.

That got me to thinking about how I've been all this time. I mean, how would I know what Alex feels like unless I tried some of that stuff myself? Maybe it makes you feel lousy the next day, but people do it because it's worth it. If it wasn't worth it, why would they go to the trouble? But Alex is not your ordinary kind of person. She says things and does things that nobody else can get away with. Like the time when she told a teacher she didn't want to take a test because she already knew she didn't know any of the answers, so why

waste the time? And the teacher had to agree with her because what she said made so much sense! If anyone else did that, they'd be in detention hall every day for the rest of their lives! I thought maybe I should strike out and be bolder, like Alex.

But then I thought of Uncle Ray sitting on the front steps with his head in his hands because he's so ashamed of the way he looks. Maybe that's just from drinking though.

If Alex wasn't going to talk to me, how could I get along at school? Nobody seems to be friendly. Not even the girls in the sports program. They look at me like I'm something from outer space. Half of them are into ballet and yoga so they'll fit into their clothes better. The other half don't care what they look like, and they stare at me like if I try to talk to them they'll kill me and eat me. In the morning on the way to science class, I see bunches of people standing outside in the hall talking and laughing and having a good old time. But not me. I have to stand way back and just watch them carry on. Or get out of the hall until just before class time and then sneak into the room, not so early that everybody can see me sitting as they walk in, and not so late that I'm the one who has to face them when I walk in.

The ones who seem to have the most fun are the Heads, the ones Alex hangs out with all the time. They wear the craziest stuff, like they don't care what you think of them. I'd like to be like that, I mean when it comes to not caring what people think. The problem with the Heads is that they are always in trouble with the teacher. They don't do their homework, or they talk right in the middle of a test because they are just not doing it. I don't want that kind of trouble. I need good grades to get a scholarship. If you get good grades, you can't be a Head because you'd probably get picked on for being a teacher's pet or something. This whole thing bothers me so much. I wish I could just forget about all of it. Except that I keep thinking that I should apologize to

Alex for whatever I said to make her mad. Maybe I should even show up at her party. I've already got my parents thinking that I might go. They don't like the idea, but they think it is more normal to be around other kids than to stay home and read. And ever since I tried to change the light bulb for Mom, we haven't got along as well as we used to. She's had a funny look on her face like she's out to get me. She's watching me like a hawk.

So I called Alex up on Saturday morning. I didn't want to sound too wimpy, so I said, "I'm coming over to help set up your place for tonight."

"Whatever, man," she said, and hung up on me. I skipped my workout that morning so I could help her out. Mom was surprised that I wasn't on my way to the courts. She acted like it was a good thing for me to be going over to a friend's house rather than to be running and practicing volleys. Dad was working on a big project at the plant. They were finishing up a bomb project, and since he's the boss he had to be there when everybody worked overtime. I was glad he was gone because I kind of felt guilty going over to Alex's knowing that I might do something he wouldn't approve of. I felt as if I was telling a lie, even though I hadn't told one yet. I guess if you know you are about to do something wrong, it's okay to start feeling bad for it in advance. It doesn't make it better, but it's something, anyway.

I got to Alex's just as she was leaving. She had her book bag strapped to her back, and it was all sagged out like it was empty.

"Let's go," she said.

"Where to?"

"To get some more junk for the party. You're helping, right?" Alex had skinny legs, but she walked real fast so I had to practically skip to keep up with her. "I figure we'll need at least one more six pack and some proof, maybe a couple of those."

"Proof?"

"You know, like high-octane party fuel." Then she smiled at me and said, "I'm glad you're along for the ride, Deonna."

"Me, too," I said. I thought she meant that she wasn't mad at me anymore. But that's not what she meant.

"Yeah, you can distract the guy behind the counter while I do a little grocery shopping."

"Why?"

Alex stopped dead in her tracks. She put her hands on her hips. There were glittery stars painted on her fingernails, and a few of them were reflecting the sun into my eyes. She was definitely mad again. "When were you born? Yesterday? We can't just go BUY the stuff, you know. When we get there, you charm his pants off. Like talk about antacids or something he'll probably know a lot about. Talk a lot so I can get the stuff into my bag. Count to twenty real slow before you come out after me."

"You can't steal! You'll get caught!"

Alex started walking real fast. "If I get caught, well, you just run after me and pretend to be my nursemaid and tell 'em that I have this disease that makes me steal and that I can't help it. Then give 'em back the stuff and apologize all over the place."

"You expect them to believe me?"

"I don't expect to get caught in the first place. And if you're chicken, you'll give off chicken vibes. You'll wreck everything. Even the party. Don't put chicken vibes in the booze, Deonna, ya hear?"

As we were going into the store, this guy from our school who plays some of the best tennis I've ever seen came out of the store ripping open a pack of bubble gum. This guy was famous at school for blowing giant green bubbles while he played. You're not supposed to chew gum on the courts and especially during a game, but he's so good, nobody says anything to him. I personally would never have the guts to say

anything to him. He's real built, and he'd never even say boo to me. But Alex walked right up to him and wrapped her long, freckled arm around his big shoulders.

"Hey ya sport-o, how's it goin'?"

"Alex! You still doing it tonight?"

"Got it. And bring some of your sport-o friends, Dave. I like to mix it up a little, ya know."

Dave gave Alex a flashy smile and then looked me up and down. "Who's the friend?"

"This is Deonna. She's helping out, if ya know what I mean."

"I'd hang around too, but I gotta run. See ya tonight, you animal, and bring your friend." Then he starting running slowly down the street, chomping on his gum. He turned around and winked at me just before he ran across the street. "And hey, your friend there has an incredible serve, Alex. Really boffo." He made a smooth, powerful circle with his arm and mimicked what I do when I serve up a sure ace.

"What a dude, huh?" Alex said.

"He's a friend of yours? I didn't know you liked jocks."

"I don't. But Dave's more than a jock. He's the key to my future."

I had a secret hope that maybe Dave liked me. Then I thought, no way. How could a big, hunky white guy who runs the whole show on the varsity team go after a dinky little black girl who hasn't even made her mark yet? But then, how did he know about my serve? And what about his knowing what we were going into the liquor store to do? You'd never think to look at him that he was like Alex that way.

"Time's a-wastin', Deonna. Let's get the stuff and get outta here."

"But..."

"But nothin'. You either get in there and smile like you're all teeth at that counter guy, or get lost. I'm gettin' pretty

tired of all this, really!" Alex's eyes were shiny, as if all her anger floated up into them and shone like moons.

"Okay, I guess. Let's go," I said, but I knew as soon as I swung open the glass door and started smiling that I never should have gone along with Alex in the first place.

Chapter Six

The guy behind the counter didn't look so big when we walked into the store, but it was like he got bigger and hairier and fatter the closer I got. Alex split off into the section where all the foot pads and bandages were and it was just me and this big guy up in the front. I stood in front of him and squinted at the shelves behind him where the cigarettes were kept. I tried to look interested in finding something.

"You can't smoke, you're too young," the guy said in a booming voice. He had kind of a scraggly beard. I could picture him riding one of those giant motorcycles with the front forks all stretched out on the road. The kind of guy who wore chains instead of a shirt, maybe with one of those World War I helmets instead of a regular motorcycle helmet. His arms had tattoos on them that looked like someone poked a blue ball point pen into his skin a few times to make one of those happy smiling faces. But he didn't look like a smiley face sort of a guy.

"I left my glasses at home. I'm looking for something to settle my stomach," I said. Inside my head, I was praying, "Come on, Alex, get a move on. Get it over with, let's go!"

"Got a little tummy ache, huh? Well, the antacids are just over there. You gotcha Tums, gotcha Rolaids and these new ones that make a foam when you bite 'em. What'll you have,

young lady?" His eyes were jet black. His eyes made my eyes look yellow they were so dark. They were scary, and they were everywhere.

"Uh, I can't decide. Let me think about it a minute." I walked back and forth in front of the display. I thought of buying something and leaving. Alex would have to get out of this mess herself. This guy gave me the creeps. He could split me in two with a little squeeze. This is just plain wrong! I don't do things like this. Why am I doing this? I thought.

Then a cop came through the glass front doors and walked in wearing the whole outfit, including the hat. I thought I was going to faint or turn green right on the spot.

"Hey, Moe! How goes it today?" said the cop as he walked past me to the coffee pots.

I thought, oh God, oh God, get me out of here. Something's about to happen, I just know it, I can feel it like I can feel the goosebumps on my arms. Where was Alex? I picked up a handful of antacids and brought them over to the part of the counter next to the cash register.

"You want all of these? Maybe you got the flu, lady." The counter guy bent down to look at my face. "You don't look well. You're a little sweaty. Let me see."

Just like Mom does, he put his wrist to my forehead to see if I had a temperature. He put his other hand on the back of my head to make sure he got a good measurement. For a big guy, he sure was gentle. His dark eyes didn't look so scary anymore. I wanted to whisper to him something to get me out of what was about to happen. I wanted to say something like, "Look back there. See that girl ripping off wine and beer? She's going to walk out the door with it, then turn around and walk back in. She's got this mental disease. Don't bust her. She's harmless." But I didn't do that. Instead, I said, "I'm okay, I'll just go home and rest or something."

"You do that," he said, kindly. "You kids run yourselves

down all the time. I remember how I used to..."

"Moe, hey Moe," the cop brought his coffee cup with a white lid on it over to the counter. "Take a look in the mirror. Back there, by the fridge section."

"I'll pay for one of these now," I said, trying to distract him for a second, but then the cop looked down at me and pulled his sunglasses low on his nose and took a long look at my face. The counter guy looked up in the mirror, then slowly walked around the counter and out toward the rows of diapers and school supplies. Why wasn't he headed straight for Alex?

"Hey, don't you play tennis at the high school?" the cop asked me. My heart was pounding so hard, I was afraid to look up at his face and afraid to speak.

"Uh huh," I managed to say.

"You've got a mean serve. I've never seen anyone with a serve like that. I went out on a Saturday a couple of weekends ago to watch my son practice, and I saw you putting them away like you were playing badminton."

"GOTCHA!" yelled the counter guy from the back. I couldn't see what was going on, but then there was a shuffling noise and then a crash like bottles smashing and spilling. The cop stomped toward the noise in his big black shoes. His legs were bowed. I was up in front all by myself. I thought, I could make a mad dash for the door and be home before anyone had a chance to know I was part of this thing. But then it hit me like a ton of bricks; that cop knew where I went to school. He even knew I was a tennis player. He could find me in a second and bust me! I froze at the front of the store, waiting for them to come out of the rows of food and other stuff. I heard Alex grunt and scream and say, "Damn pigs." The cop marched Alex out toward the front counter with the counter guy right behind her, carrying an empty book bag that was soaked all the way through by something that smelled a little fruity. Alex's eyes were wild like

some crazy animal's eyes.

"Whoa, whoa there, little girl," said the cop, as he yanked Alex's arms up behind her by pulling on the handcuffs.

"That's free coffee for you today, Jack. Thanks. Don't be breaking the kid's arms, now," said the counter guy, who stood in front of Alex with his chunky, hairy arms crossed.

"Caught her hitting the cherry wine in the back, Moe. She got scared when she saw me and dropped it all over that back pack. I'll pay for it."

"Don't even think about it. As long as she didn't carry anything off, that's what matters."

Alex was looking down at the ground. I guess that's the only place she could look, considering her arms were behind her back and the cop still had them raised up so she couldn't stand up straight. "I didn't do anything bad. I'll pay for the wine, I swear. You're hurting me," she said. Her voice sounded high and shaky, like she was scared.

"You think I care about a $2.95 bottle of cheap wine? You think I care about the money? You've got some news coming to you, kid. I care about how come you're sneaking drinks, that's what. You're fifteen, sixteen at the most. You got a problem?" The counter guy waved his hand at the cop to tell him to let her arms down so she could look up, but Alex kept her eyes aimed at the floor. Her hair covered her face.

"If this were my son, I'd make him sorry he was ever born. Thank God my boy doesn't do any of this stuff," the cop said. "He's hooked on tennis and that's all he's hooked on."

If I could only see her face, I'd know what to say. I was leaning on the counter to stop myself from shaking. Would we both get in trouble? Would they let her go? Was I supposed to know her if we got caught, or pretend that we never saw each other?

"I said, do you have some kind of problem?" The counter guy's voice got angrier and louder. Now he looked as scary

as I thought he did when I first came into the store.

"No," said Alex in a quiet whisper.

"What would your folks say if we gave them a call right now, I wonder?" said the cop.

"There's only my mother. Nobody knows where my father is," she said.

"A broken home. I thought so. They're all the same," the cop said to the counter guy. "So how about we call your mother right now?"

"You can't. She's a flight attendant and she's in Hawaii somewhere." Alex looked at me with a dumb look on her face. I didn't know what to make of it.

"And a teenage latchkey kid, to boot," said the cop, and he rubbed the end of his blond mustache like he was thinking about what he should do with her. Then he turned to me. "You know her?"

"No, sir," I said, trying to make it sound as if I really didn't.

"I don't know, Moe. What do you think? It isn't serious, at least for you, anyway," the cop said.

"Let's get some information and let her go. If she comes into my store again, we'll nail her." The counter guy went behind the cash register and pulled up a pad of paper and a stubby pencil. "Name?"

"Alexandra Starky."

"Mother's name?" the counter guy asked, still scribbling.

"Claudia Starky," said Alex. I thought to myself, I know you, Alex. You're saying her name is Claudia, but you're thinking The Fluff, instead.

"What airline does she work for, what's your home address, and what school do you go to?" asked the cop.

Oh no, I thought. He knows what school I go to, and now he'll figure it all out. I could still make the door before he could grab me, but then he's still got Alex. He could make her tell everything. If I run, he'll figure out that we had a plan. My heart was pounding in my head so hard that I

thought I would have trouble hearing.

"Ralph Waldo Emerson High," said Alex, and quickly shot her eyes at me and then back to the counter guy's face. She lied about her school. Emerson High is our rival school, about five miles in the opposite direction from Edison. And it's a college prep school, too.

"How does someone like you get into a fine institution like that? Now this girl, she's the one who ought to be at Emerson. I swear, there's no justice in this world," said the cop.

What did he mean by that? Did he mean that someone with a good serve should be in a private school, or did he really mean that a black girl with a stomachache should be in a good school and a white girl who drinks cheap booze should be in a mixed-up regular school? I wanted to tell him that we were both in the exact same high school and to let my friend go. But I just stared at Alex and the cop.

The cop took off the handcuffs and gave Alex a shove toward the door. "You hightail it out of here and don't ever let Moe see your face in his store again. He sees your face, and you're in mucho trouble. Have I made that clear enough for you, or are you just a dumb drunk who has to learn the hard way? Now get out of here."

Alex grabbed her wet book bag from Moe's hand and walked out the door and down the street. She didn't even look back to see if I was following her.

The counter guy turned to me and wiped some sweat off of the tip of his nose. "You need to get home, little lady, and get yourself some rest. You don't need any of this stuff. Maybe some soup or something, but not his." He scooped all the antacids off the counter into one of his tattooed hands like it was a shovel. I was still shaking and trying to control my pounding heart when I said good-bye and walked out of the store. As I got to the door, I heard the cop say to Moe, "Well, at least that redhead wasn't on something harder than berry juice."

"They all seem to be on something," said Moe.

"You know that black girl's got a great serve. I saw her play tennis when I went to watch my son..." The cop's voice was all I heard once the doors closed behind me. It was all I could do not to run away from there. But where? To Alex's to see how she was? As I started to calm down, I was so mad at Alex for getting me into a situation like that that I almost wanted to get revenge. I wanted to make her feel as sick and full of fear as I did when she made me go into that store knowing full well we were going to rip Moe off. But I ran home instead. I flew past Dad, who was watching TV, and didn't say anything when Mom called out my name as I ran past her room. I jumped into bed and pulled the pillow over my head. I felt confused about what had happened, and had prickly feelings like even though we weren't caught and sent to jail, we could have been if Alex had put even one bottle into her book bag. Everything could have been ruined right there. Nothing would have ever been the same for me ever again.

"Deonna, what's the matter?" Mom barged into my room and came up to my bed.

"Nothing's wrong. Just a headache, that's all," I said. But I wanted to tell her so bad...tell her everything that happened that morning and that I was sorry and I'd never do it again. I wasn't used to acting sick when I was fine. Somehow I was lying again, even if I didn't want to. But even while Mom made me turn over so she could feel my forehead to see if I had a temperature just like Moe had done, I knew it would be a long time before I would ever get up the guts to tell anyone what nearly happened to me in that store.

"If you're not feeling well, you're not going to that party you wanted to go to," Mom said.

I didn't bother to answer her. I just turned my face into the pillow and said, " So what?"

Chapter Seven

From my room, I could hear voices in the front of the house. It sounded like Aunt Martha and Uncle Ray. But they usually didn't visit at the same time. Nobody said they were going to come over that day, so it was a big surprise for Mom and Dad. I went down the hall past the bedrooms expecting to see Uncle Ray like he usually is, crumpled up and smelly with his hair matted down and his clothes all torn and wrinkled. But that's not how he looked at all! It had been a long time since I had seen him in daylight, because he usually came to our house after everyone was in bed asleep. At first I thought something bad was going to happen and that when I went into the living room they would tell me that they were going to get a divorce or something, but that isn't how it happened.

The first thing I saw was Uncle Ray, wearing a big smile and a small straw hat with a red band around the top. He had on a white jacket with little red stripes running up and down it, and a pair of white pants with sharp creases. He even had on a pair of shiny white shoes. That wasn't the Uncle Ray that I was used to seeing!

Aunt Martha was pushing Uncle Ray into the dining room and telling him to sit down so they could talk to Mom and Dad. She usually dressed pretty good, but this time it looked

like she was going to a fashion show for older ladies. She had on this flowy yellow skirt and a little shiny blouse with all sorts of tiny birds on it. Her hair looked more silvery than gray and black, like it usually did. She was smiling so hard that her face was one big bunch of deep lines. I don't think I had ever seen her act so excited before.

"What's the special occasion?" Dad asked.

Aunt Martha looked at Uncle Ray and he looked back at her and smiled. His smiling at her was something new, too.

"You tell them, sugar," he said, as he took off his straw hat.

"Well, we just sold our house," Aunt Martha said.

"You what! Then where will you live?" Mom looked a little upset.

"Now you've got to hear the whole story before you go jumping to conclusions," said Uncle Ray to Mom.

"That's right, honey, you got to hear them out." Dad looked like he knew something funny was going to happen.

"You know, Ray and I have had our troubles. We've been going at it like cats and dogs for several years. He'd run off and get drunk and I'd kick him out, then he'd tell me he'd never do it again and I'd let him back in. It's been nothing but promises, promises, promises. It went on like that right up until last month. It was last month, wasn't it, Ray?" Aunt Martha reached over and touched Uncle Ray's hand.

"Nope. It was exactly eighty-eight days ago, to be exact," he said to her.

"That's right. I've been enjoying you so much, that time has just flown right by," Aunt Martha turned to Mom, Dad, and me and winked "Time flies when you're having fun!"

Mom kept staring at Uncle Ray. She said, "I can't believe how good you look, Ray! I don't think I've ever seen you look so...so...".

"Healthy?" answered Uncle Ray. "Yep. Healthy, that's me to a T. Martha's trying to tell you that I gave up drinking and finally did something good for myself."

"He hasn't had a drop since just after he stayed with you

the last time. Isn't that wonderful? And he's been going to AA meetings every single day ever since. Sometimes I go with him. They have all different kinds of meetings, and they hold them over at the church. We don't even have to drive."

"That is truly something, Martha," Mom said. "But what do they do at Alcoholics Anonymous that's so great? And how come you sold your house, that's what I want to know."

Uncle Ray laughed and said, "All in good time, all in good time."

"What's great about it is that we have a life together again. And any time Ray gets tempted, even a little bit, he can call up this man they call his sponsor and they can talk it out so that Ray feels better not having a drink than having one."

"See, I have a disease. I have no control over how much I drink. Once I start, there's just no stopping. So now I can't even have one drink. Not one. Looking back, I can't figure out how your Aunt Martha put up with me. Or you, either," said Uncle Ray, looking at me and Dad.

"Ah, Ray, you know we love you, man, no matter what kind of a bum you were," Dad said. He seemed all choked up. His eyes were shiny like he might start to cry. Dad never cried in front of me before!

I said, "How come you're all dressed up? It's only Saturday. Do you go to church on Saturday now too?"

Both Aunt Martha and Uncle Ray laughed out loud. "You know how casual we are. We only get this dressed up for weddings," said Aunt Martha. Uncle Ray grabbed her hand and held it on top of the table. He was smiling like a crazy man.

"Oh. When do you have to be at the wedding?" said Mom, looking at the clock on the wall. "We don't want to make you late. Maybe you could come back and finish your story after the reception."

"This IS the reception, and it's just about over," laughed Uncle Ray.

"No, it's just begun, my love," Aunt Martha said, looking

at Uncle Ray with goo-goo eyes. I thought to myself, "This can't be for real, can it?"

"All right, all right. Now just what is going on here? First you show up at our door by surprise at a normal hour of the day, which is a little bit strange. But look at you! You're all dressed up! Then you tell us you've sold your house but we don't know why. You've lived in that house nearly fifteen years! You're a San Francisco institution by now. Next thing you know, you're up and leaving to run off to some afternoon wedding. It just doesn't fit, and I want to know what's up." Dad wasn't really angry, but I think he was frustrated because we were getting so many different messages from Aunt Martha and Uncle Ray.

"We just got married again this morning!" Aunt Martha was smiling even wider now.

"Yep, we went and tied the knot all over again, but this time we did it even tighter, right, honey?" said Uncle Ray.

"That's right. It was just us, the minister, and two witnesses. And now we're going to elope!"

"Elope! You can't elope!" Dad said.

"Why can't they?" I asked.

"You don't just up and sell your house and elope right out in the middle of your life. That's something crazy kids do when they don't have any better sense not to," said my dad.

"I think it sounds very romantic, actually," said Mom.

"It's not the middle of our life, Mal. It's the beginning," said Uncle Ray. "We got so tied up in doing what we thought we were supposed to do that we never took time for a real honeymoon. And seeing as how I sobered up and decided that the lady I was already married to was a real humdinger, I decided to marry her all over again...and start from scratch, just like newlyweds." Uncle Ray was talking to Dad, but he was looking at Aunt Martha.

"One of the things I had to learn when I went to AA was that all I could do was forgive Ray. Otherwise, we'd never

make it. But the one thing I could never forgive him for, and he knows this, is that he was drunk as a skunk when we first got married. It hurt my feelings so badly to think that unless he didn't know it was happening, he couldn't marry me. I forgave him for all sorts of things, but that one, well, that one I just couldn't honestly forgive him for. The more I pushed him to try to get him to love me, the more he made himself scarce by getting drunk."

Uncle Ray continued by interrupting Aunt Martha. "That's entirely true, every word. I never knew I said the words "I do" until two weeks later when I opened my eyes and there I was, lying on a strange couch I thought I never saw before. But Martha and me, we went shopping for that couch and picked it out ourselves. I just never remembered doing it! So I promised to marry Martha again this time... and do it with all my heart."

"But what happened to make everything change, Ray? I mean after all these years, can an old dog really learn new tricks?"

"I'm sitting right here to prove it. What happened was, about a week after I had tried to dry out over here, I blew it and went out on a drunk again."

"And as usual," added Aunt Martha, " I told him not to bother coming back."

"But something happened this time. I mean to tell you that I was pretty embarrassed the time before that when little Deonna here had to see me in such a state. But bad as I felt about it later that week, it wasn't enough to stop me from doing it again. It was really out of hand. So I went off to my favorite watering hole and tried to get stinking drunk to forget how I felt about getting that way in the first place. But the more I tried, the less it seemed to work. I mean, I was high as a kite, but I still felt too much. I was mad about everything, even though I can't remember exactly what made me mad in the first place. The bar closed, and I knew I

couldn't go home, so I took a walk until I found an all-night liquor store. I bought one of those giant bottles with the glass carrying handle on it, you know the kind. I started into that while I walked. I didn't care where. Just as I was starting to feel pretty good, I came to the naval shipyard where I used to work when I was in school. Nobody was around, so I plunked myself down under a giant winch, and I guess I passed out. But then I woke up again, just as the sun was coming up over the Oakland hills. It was so bright it would have woken up an Egyptian mummy. Then streaks from the sun went through some gray clouds and I thought it was God giving me some kind of a sign. Inside my head, though I was probably still drunk as all get out, I kept thinking, 'It's a new day, Ray. This is your chance.' Then I got sick. I mean I got so sick I thought I was going to die right then and there. My heart felt like it was going to jump out of me and keep on running. I swear sweat was dripping off my nose like a running faucet. I took that like another sign from above. I knew if I kept up like I had been, I was going to die. But what really did it was when a night watchman came out of the guard house. There I was, sicker than a dog, having these revelations about dying, and this guy who was a carbon copy of myself came out in a crumpled-up uniform. He was in a bad way, I tell you! I thought it couldn't have been me just imagining things, because he fell down. He was a mess, just as bad as me, if not worse. He got back up and tried to get to me. I thought maybe I'm in big trouble, but I couldn't get myself up to get away. Then he fell down again, got up, and I saw that he wasn't even looking at me. He was looking at that big bottle of scotch whiskey that was right next to my leg. He was trying to get at it like a thirsty man in a desert. But the more he tried to get to the bottle, the less able he was to walk or even crawl to it. Then I put my hands over my eyes so I wouldn't have to look at his face. It was so ugly. I mean coyote ugly, it was that bad. Except that when I closed

my eyes and clamped my hand over my face, the guy just kept trying to get closer to me. I knew then that it wasn't really happening. That man in the guard house was really me. I was seeing myself and it was really something else, I mean to tell you. I knew that if I let him reach me, if I gave him my bottle, that would be the end of him. I knew I'd have to kill him. So I said out loud, "Please God, forgive me, but I've got to do it. I've got to kill myself or I'm going to kill ME." Now you may not know what I mean by that, but I knew that God certainly understood it. I got up real slow and held the bottle over my head. I aimed as best I could at the night watchman. Then I threw it as hard as I've ever thrown anything, and it went like a shot at his head. He grabbed it like it was a football. He went for it on a dive, and you know what? He just kept going, straight into the pavement. So that's what happened, in a nutshell. I killed myself. I mean, I killed that drunk in the guard house who was half me and half what I was going to be, even though I knew he didn't really exist. I saw myself and decided right then and there that I wanted to see another sunrise as beautiful as the one I woke up to that morning at the naval shipyard."

"Wow," was all I could say. Dad just stared at Uncle Ray like he couldn't believe what he had just heard.

"It was a miracle," Mom said, looking at Aunt Martha.

"Then Ray came home a couple of days later, all clean and neat as he usually did when he would come back from staying with you. Except I noticed something was different. You know how tired and sick he always looked after about the third day of drying out? Well, when he came to the door, he rang the bell, and when I went to it, there he was standing, smiling and holding a handful of wild roses. My heart stopped just like it did the first time he came to court me so long ago. Getting married again was his idea. He said he wanted to take me for his lawful wedded wife in health, and he wanted to be awake the entire time." Aunt Martha clasped

her hands to her chest and sighed.

"But what about your house?" asked Mom, for the second time.

"Oh, we took care of that. Everybody come with me," said Uncle Ray, and he stood up proud and tall and walked with big steps to the front door. We all went to the porch and looked out. "Feast your eyes on our new home, over there," he said, as he pointed with his straw hat to a spot down the street.

"That's not a home, that's a tanker, man!" said Dad.

"Oh, you two can't be serious. Can you?" Mom walked further onto the porch to get a better look at the long, shiny aluminum motor home that took up three parking spaces.

"We call it 'The Second Sunrise'," said Uncle Ray.

"And we came to say good-bye for a while. We're taking a honeymoon," said Aunt Martha.

"Yep, a long, long honeymoon. Wherever we feel like stopping, we'll stop. There's nothing to keep us from living anywhere and everywhere we want to," said Uncle Ray.

"Of course, at AA they said it's not a great idea to change your whole life so soon after you become sober, but we have a list of places we can go to attend meetings almost anywhere in the States we wander," said Aunt Martha.

"And we will go every day, just like we've been doing here," Uncle Ray said.

Mom and Dad just stared at the motor home like it was a spaceship from another galaxy. Nobody said anything for a while, so I said, "Well, I'm glad you're going."

"Deonna! How rude! We'll miss your aunt and uncle terribly," said Mom.

"I'll miss them, too, Mom," I said to her, then smiled at both of them.

"But you know that wherever we are, we'll always be thinking about you, don't you? asked Aunt Martha.

"Uh huh," I said, " I meant that I'm glad you're going

because I was really getting tired of changing Uncle Ray's sheets all the time."

Uncle Ray bent over and gave me a kiss on top of my head, and then added a big bear hug. He smelled like shaving cream and spicy cologne. He said, "I'm sorry I was such a lousy example of an uncle to you. I hope you'll find it in your heart to forgive me for causing you so much extra trouble, Deonna." Then Uncle Ray and Aunt Martha hugged and kissed us all good-bye. Mom started to cry, and I thought she ran into the house to get a tissue. But then she came out just as Aunt Martha was pulling the motor home away from the curb. Mom had tears in her eyes, but she started laughing and brought a big sack of rice out from behind her back and started throwing it.

Mom and Dad stood next to me with their arms around one another, and we watched Aunt Martha drive that round, shiny new house of theirs all the way to the end of our street. When she made a right turn to get out to the main boulevard that led to the freeway, we could still see Uncle Ray's bright smile sticking out from under that little straw hat.

"A real miracle," Dad said.

"I think I'm going to cry again," Mom told him, as they walked back into the house.

"It made me feel pretty good, too," I said.

"Oh? I thought you weren't feeling very well," Mom said.

But I felt great. If Uncle Ray could change his life like that, then I knew that anything was possible. I ran into my room to let Alex know that I'd be at her party that night. She acted like nothing had happened earlier that day at the liquor store. Maybe like Uncle Ray, she just couldn't remember it.

Chapter Eight

After my aunt and uncle left for their honeymoon, I felt pretty inspired. I went to the court and served up about a hundred balls. Almost every one would have been a smoking ace if I were playing a real game. Then I came home and put on some jeans and my favorite sweatshirt and sneakers. I told Mom before I left that I didn't want any dinner because there would be food at the party.

"That's good. If there's lots of food, that means there probably won't be a lot of other shenanigans going on besides loud music. I know what parties are all about, you know," she said.

"And guess what? There's this guy who is on our varsity tennis team and I think he likes me. He'll be at the party." When I said that, Mom's face lit up like a sixty-watt bulb. I knew if she thought I would be hanging around with a guy, she'd be happy enough to stop worrying about what kids do at parties. But the truth was that I really was pretty happy to get a chance to see Dave again.

When I got to Alex's apartment, I had to let myself in because nobody was answering the bell. The place was loaded with people and it was only 8:30. I had thought that one of these parties would look really colorful with balloons and

streamers and lots of finger food and stuff. But Alex didn't put up any special decorations. It was smoky and noisy and really hot, and I had to push and shove and get in between people to get to the kitchen where I thought I'd find my friend. But she wasn't in the kitchen. There were about six kids I had never seen around the kitchen table. I couldn't see what they were doing because their heads were all bent in close together, so I went closer and stood on tiptoes. I thought maybe it was a board game or something.

"Hey! Back off," yelled this little guy, who was chopping up white powder with a razor blade in a glass baking dish. I remembered seeing him in school. Everybody called him the "little Napoleon." They said he'd be a great lawyer someday because all he cared about was getting people set up for big fights and then making money from taking bets on who would win.

"Whoa, sor-ree. Kick me for living!" I said to him, as he put one hand into his inside jacket pocket and brought out a straw. I thought, as I walked away, that his nickname was perfect for him. Now I knew what they were doing, and I didn't want to be anyplace where I wasn't welcome, so I pushed my way out of the kitchen to find Alex.

From the living room I could see the top of the front door open and then all these people started making noise and looking at the people coming into the room. It was Dave! I thought to myself, down girl, don't get nervous. I shoved through the crowd to get a better look. Dave showed up with three other guys. They were all wearing our school colors on their nylon warm-up suits. Everybody else looked like trash beside them. Dave was slapping people on the back and talking while he tried to take off his jacket. He looked like he wanted to put it somewhere but couldn't find a place. So I popped over to him and said, "I'll find a place to put that for you."

"Hey, it's you! What are you doing here?" he said.

"Just hanging out, I guess."

"You seen Alex? I'm in the mood for some major partying."

"I'm looking for her myself. Maybe she's in her room. Want me to show you?" I couldn't believe I was talking to him. The greatest guy on the team, the best-looking one that everybody thought was so hot, was hanging out with me, Deonna Johnson, the nobody. I got in front of him and pushed through the crowd to the hall. It wasn't hard, because everybody seemed to get out of Dave's way real fast. I opened the linen closet in the hall and shoved Dave's jacket in so nobody would take it. Alex's bedroom door was closed. I knocked, but nobody answered. The music and voices were so loud that probably nobody could have heard me if I'd screamed. Dave just turned the doorknob and walked right in ahead of me like he had been in Alex's room a million times before.

Four people were sitting on the edge of Alex's bed and three others on the floor. Nobody seemed to notice us. The place smelled partly like a butcher shop, kind of metallic, and then sort of like rubber and burnt matches. Alex was there on the floor with her knees bent and her head resting on her arms. You couldn't see her face at all.

"Great! You guys are already kickin' it," Dave said, and sat down on the floor next to Alex. "Hey dude, you got a killer bash goin' on here. Put me down for some niblets."

Dude? Alex was a dude? I thought, wow, I've got lots to learn from hanging out at this party. One guy dropped a few little white pebbles into a plastic pipe and lit it until it glowed. He put his mouth on the top of the pipe and inhaled. You could see the smoke go straight up the pipe and into his mouth. Then he passed it over to Dave. That must have been the guy named Rabbit that Alex was talking about, because he had a face that looked just like one. Rabbit put his hands on the floor like he was trying to brace himself so

he wouldn't fall over. His eyes rolled back into his head and all you could see were the bloodshot whites.

I sat down next to Alex. "Alex, it's me, are you okay?" She still hadn't moved from her balled-up position on the floor.

"Nuhhh. Bug someone else. Naa me." Alex was too far gone even to talk. But I thought, so what? I could at least try to talk to Dave here where it wasn't as crowded. But Dave wasn't into talking to me at all.

Dave took a deep drag on the pipe and acted like he was going to heaven. He said, "Aya!" Then the handed the pipe to me. I had to think fast. Now what do I do? I didn't want to put my mouth on some filthy pipe that everyone else had already slobbered over, and I didn't know what I would feel like if I tried it. I had already heard stories about some people at school who only did it once and just dropped dead. I knew that you could get hooked from doing coke even a little bit. And I had to always stay in top form so that I could make the team next semester. No team, no scholarship, no college, no professional career. I could see it all right in front of me, but I didn't want to look stupid in front of Dave. I thought, well, it doesn't seem to bother his game to do this stuff. I just didn't want to get messed up by accident and miss out on my big chance.

"It's not so burly, you know. Here!" Dave shoved the pipe into my hands.

"I can't. I'm training," I said, shrugging my shoulders. I thought that of all the people in the world, he would know how important that would be. I mean there he was, the best tennis player anywhere. He should know enough not to even smoke cigarettes. But this stuff was worse.

I felt pretty stupid just holding the pipe in my hand. Nobody else in the room seemed really anxious to take it from me, either.

"You're fresh out of church or something, huh?" said

Dave with a mean look on his face.

"No, but this stuff could kill you and you know it."

"Go back to Mommy and Daddy then. Go back to your little dollhouse. I thought you were Alex's friend, and Alex likes to do a little base now and then, don't you, Alex?"

Alex didn't answer him.

"I am her friend," I said, "but I don't think it's funny to keep giving this stuff to her when she's already a wreck." I was getting mad.

Alex put her hand on my arm. It was cold and clammy. She was trying to say something. Finally, after a few tries, she raised her head and looked at me. "I'm sa' fine, Deonna. No pain. Dave's a sport-o. Be nice to him, ya' hear?"

"I'm not faced," Dave said. "Give it to Alex, Deonna. She looks like she could use a little more."

"I don't think so," I said. Alex's head dropped back down on her knees, and her hand was starting to shake. She reminded me of how Uncle Ray looked the last time he came to our house to dry out. Then Alex raised her head like nothing was the matter and said, "Let's go for a drive!"

"Now you're talkin', dude! Let's go!" Dave helped Alex up. All of a sudden Alex started acting like she was a wound-up toy or something. "And let's take Deonna with us," she added, "she never gets to have any fun, right?"

"I don't know if that's a good idea right now," I said. I was thinking, you're so loaded you can't even see straight. How're you going to drive a car?

"We're going, and that's that," Dave said. "And besides, it'll be a chance to get some fresh air. These other dudes are real goobers."

So whether I wanted to or not, we all went to the back of the apartment building where Alex's mom had her car parked.

"You sure you can drive?" I saw Alex walking funny, then walking normal, then looking all around her like she was be-

ing followed. But it was only Rabbit, Dave, me and her.

"Alex is a great driver. Real fast. She can make this old clunker go eighty in no time," Dave said.

Everybody climbed into the car except me. "What's the problem, Deonna? I'm fine, really, I'm fine. We're just gonna grease the wheels a little bit."

"I think I better go home," I said. I was afraid to get into the car. It gave me the creeps to think about going fast when the driver only had a learner's permit and was high from free-basing. I thought I'd better get back into my own house and forget that I ever knew these people at all.

Then Dave got out of the car and put his big hands on my shoulders. "Look, Deonna, it's only a car. It's only a little drive. Nothing's going to happen. Anyway, if we get a speeding ticket, my dad's a cop. He'll take care of it, he always does."

I was afraid to move because I didn't want him to take his hands off my shoulders. "Your dad's a cop?"

"Yeah, do you know him?" Dave asked.

"Well, me and Alex might have met him this morning. Remember that cop this morning?" I turned to Alex.

"What cop? When? I don't hang out with cops, no way." Alex revved the engine. "Will ya make up your mind already? My foot's dyin' to get it on with these cute little pedals, ya know?"

Dave looked at me like I was something really scummy and got into the car. He closed the door and rolled down his window. "Catch you later, man." Alex backed out of the carport and spun the car around in a circle like it was out of control. They peeled rubber for about fifty yards. Dave stuck his upper body out of the window and yelled back at me, "Much, much later, man!"

I felt like crud. I walked around the corner and started for home. I remember thinking that I'd never be able to show my face at school again, because Dave would laugh at me if

he ever saw me again. Or Alex wouldn't hang out with me anymore. Or maybe everyone at that party would think I was some kind of a baby. I didn't want to cry, but I felt my eyes and nose swell up. How come they didn't care about what happened to them? What was so lousy about their lives that they wanted to fry their brains to a crisp with that coke stuff? It didn't look good, and it smelled worse. If it made you pass out and then act like an idiot, what good was it? But that wasn't why I started to cry. I was crying because I just felt like a total freak of nature. Maybe I should listen to Mom and stop working out so much. Or give up trying to be a famous tennis player. What good would it do me to be the best in the world if I was bound to be lonely all my life? I thought I should loosen up more. Maybe go back to the party and try it all out at once to see how I liked it. And then, all of a sudden, about three blocks away from Alex's building, I saw two cars coming really fast down the middle of the street. One of them was Alex's car! She was racing with a carload of screaming guys, and it looked like she was pulling ahead of them. But then I saw the other car bump Alex's car. Everything that happened after that moved in slow motion. I still can't believe I saw it all happen.

The other car bumped Alex's car on the driver's side and sent it skidding sideways into a giant telephone pole. It was the metal kind, the one that connected all the wires to the smaller wooden ones. Alex's car sort of wrapped around the pole on the passenger's side. I couldn't move. I couldn't even scream. I was just trapped right where I was, and it seemed like a real long time before I snapped out of it. The guys in the other car stopped way up ahead of the pole, backed up fast, took a look at Alex's car, and then took off like there was no tomorrow. That's when I ran up to see if everything was okay. Other people came running out of their houses and started opening the doors. Rabbit climbed out of the back of the car, screaming and crying. He rolled around on

the grass next to the curb and held onto his leg. By the time I got near the car, I could hear the sound of sirens, and people were crowding around the car. I pushed people out of my way to get close enough to see if Alex was okay, but when I got through to the driver's side, Alex wasn't there!

All I remember seeing, and I don't think I'll ever be able to get it out of my head, was the way Dave's face looked. His head was turned sideways against the dashboard, and the dash and the lower part of the front windshield bulged outward in the shape of his head. His eyes were totally open. His white warm-ups were covered with blood. I couldn't even see the green stripes down the side of his pants. All I saw was blood, and the look that was on this face. He looked like a little boy who just got off a hairy roller coaster ride.

Chapter Nine

I ran back to the party to find Alex, but she wasn't there. Her place was still full of people and smoke, and the speakers were blasting so hard that they made a buzzing sound. I left her apartment and decided that I'd better go home. I didn't know where else to go or what I should do. I thought it was all some kind of a bad dream, or maybe I had gotten some of the smoke in my body and I was hallucinating. But I had never hallucinated before so I didn't know for sure.

I walked all the way home, trying to calm myself down and figure out what to do. Alex must be okay, I thought, or else she'd still be in the car. My parents would want to know how the party was, and they would read the paper tomorrow or hear about the crash. If it mentioned Alex's name somehow, they'd know I had something to do with the crash. Then they'd find out that I was at a drug party. Mom would say, "I knew it all along. You're doing drugs, just like I thought." But I wasn't doing drugs. And I didn't get into the car. And I meant to leave the party because I wasn't having any fun. If I told my parents what happened, I'd be grounded for the summer for sure. Then it would be just as bad as if I were in that car. No practice, no lessons. I'd never get on the team. That meant more to me than anything. To make the tennis team and prove I was worth looking at. What was really im-

portant, I asked myself? Taking a chance that my parents would figure out what happened outside of the party, or making the team?

My heart was beating so hard when I came up the walk to our front porch that I could hear it echoing around in my head. It was about 11:30 and all the lights were out. Mom and Dad were asleep on the couch. Dad's head was resting on Mom's lap, and a bowl of popcorn was moving up and down on Dad's big stomach every time he breathed. I tiptoed to my room and got ready for bed. But I couldn't sleep. Dave's face kept showing up every time I closed my eyes. And when I opened them to keep from seeing his bulging eyeballs looking at me, I'd think about what Alex was going to do. Where could she hide and for how long? I imagined that a cop would come to the door and tell my parents what happened. The cop would pull out a long list like it was a roll of toilet paper and read them everything I did, and all the lies I had already told them so far. And worse, there were blank spaces at the end of the roll to make room for the lies I was planning to tell if they didn't find out by themselves what happened. Somehow, I must have made myself to tired that I finally fell asleep.

On Sunday morning, I woke up before everyone else did and dialed Alex's phone number. I didn't expect her to answer the phone, but she did!

"What happened? Where were you?" I said real softly so my parents wouldn't hear me.

Alex sounded funny. She sounded like she was talking in a tunnel. All of her words came out so slowly. Sometimes she skipped whole words. "Doesn't matter. He's dead and it's all my fault. So what if it is my fault. They're going to get me. All of them. All those people...looking at me...I'm really great, aren't I."

"Sure you're great. Don't worry. Just stay cool and we'll talk about it tomorrow in school," I said to her. I knew she

was in trouble. I was so confused myself, though. If I hung up and ran over there, I'd give myself away. If I stayed on the phone, I'd get caught and wouldn't be able to help her. "I gotta go now. They're comin'...I really blew it this time. I won't let 'em get me. You won't say anything, Deonna? Promise you won't tell anyone I killed Dave. You've got to swear on a stack of bibles you won't." "I swear! I'd get in so much trouble you wouldn't even believe it. But where will you go? Who's going to get you? Isn't your mom supposed to come home today? Is someone there?" I was starting to get the idea that Alex was paranoid. I had seen her act like this before when she would party all night, but never this bad. "Nobody's here. Nobody's ever here. Everyone has someone but me," she said. "You've got me, Alex! I'm always around, you know that," I said. "Sure. You'll tell, I know you will. I'd rather die than spend my life in some stinkin' jail," she said. "It'll be rough, but it has to blow over sometime..." Alex hung up the phone while I was talking. She wouldn't really do that, I mean kill herself, would she? She wasn't the type. Alex was full of life, always ready to jump around and make noise. I sat on the edge of my bed and tried to see her running a razor blade over her white wrists, but I just couldn't picture it. I said to myself, "Nah, she'd never do it. She'd just stay stoned for the rest of her life so she wouldn't feel anything."

I decided not to tell anyone about the party or the accident or anything else unless I was caught red-handed. I decided to do it that way even though I knew I was dead wrong. Alex wouldn't say anything. She'd just clean up her apartment and be sitting there with her head between the stereo speakers like she always did when her mom came back from a flight. She'd tell her mom about the accident,

the insurance would pay for the car, and everybody would be really sorry about Dave. They'd say something over the loudspeakers about Dave at school tomorrow morning. Then everything would get back to normal again.

So I stayed quiet that day. I did everything as usual that morning, talking to my parents like nothing was wrong at all. I went out to the courts and hit flat tennis balls against the wall as hard as I could to work up a good sweat. This is what feels good, I thought as I in lay in the grass near the courts after an hour of practicing. It feels good to be alive. To see a field full of trees and grass and know that it is just that...trees and grass and not twisted, bloody faces coming to ruin your life. At my house later that evening, Mom didn't even ask me about the party. She just wondered how it went with Dave.

"Nothing happened. He was too crazy. Who needs a hyper freak hanging around them all the time?" I said.

"You're too hard on everyone. I bet you didn't give him the time of day," Mom said.

"I got bored and came home early. You guys were snoring away when I came in." My heart started beating again. I expected a cop to come to the door at any minute and take me away. Then I told myself I was acting just as paranoid as Alex.

"Well, better boring than something else. You know how those parties can get. It scares me to even think of it."

It scared me, too, but I didn't tell Mom that. I wished I could have stayed with her. I wanted to tell her everything that happened. I wanted her to say she understood that I had made some stupid mistakes and then just know that I would never do it the same way again. Every few seconds I felt my mouth start to say something and I choked it back. After all, I swore that I wouldn't, even though I wasn't sure that I could keep my promise.

Chapter Ten

At homeroom the next morning, I heard the guy who usually does the announcements say, "Now let us have five minutes of silence for Alex Starky and Dave Kingsley." A guy sitting behind me said, "I knew those guys would OD sometime." The speaker above the door crackled and then the announcement went on. "Services for Dave will be on Wednesday. Dave's father, Officer Jack Kingsley, requests that donations be sent instead of flowers to the..." The speaker crackled and went dead, and nobody in the class said a word. I ran out of the room like a shot.

I ran all the way home. I didn't care if we weren't allowed to leave the school grounds without a pass. I just ran and ran, and didn't care if I was out of breath as I climbed the hills to my house. Alex couldn't be dead! I thought she was just going to run away or something. Not die over it! I knew about Dave and it was too bad. But Alex, never! It just couldn't be!

Mom wasn't home, and I was glad at least for that. I had to figure out what to do. So I called Alex's house. Mrs. Starky answered the phone. Her voice sounded very strange, like she had a cold and was having trouble keeping her voice from shaking.

"It's me, Deonna. Is Alex home?"

"Deonna. Do you know what happened? What happened to my girl? Why did she do that to herself? I don't know, I just don't know," she said.

"What happened? What do you mean?" I thought I better figure out what Mrs. Starky knew before I opened my big mouth.

"I came home yesterday and she was unconscious. They pumped her stomach...she tried to kill herself, but she didn't die, she's just hanging on in a coma. No message, no nothing. And I can't figure out what happened. The police have been here twice today. They want to talk to Alex about this Dave she was with over the weekend. They can't tell me anything. They don't know if she'll make it."

I felt so bad for her. She didn't have a clue. "I'm really sorry," I said. "I don't know what hapened. I left her party Saturday night and that's all. Can I go see her?"

"She's at General Hospital on Potrero Street. There's nothing you can do. She's not responding to anything at all. It's like...it's like..."

"Take it easy, Mrs. Starky. I'll see Alex as soon as I can get over there," I said, and hung up the phone before I started to totally break down.

That was weeks ago. I've been in to see Alex about every other day and nothing has changed. Nobody has figured out what happened. I'm the only one who really knows.

Today I went into Alex's room again. It was quiet outside, like the whole world was waiting for something big to happen. I knew I had to do something today for sure. I couldn't just let Alex's mom keep crying. I thought about Dave's parents. They must be really bad off, too. And I couldn't live with myself anymore. I thought I was so bad for all the lying and staying quiet when I should have said something, that I couldn't sleep or eat or act normal. I kept having nightmares, seeing the crash over and over again, or seeing me try out freebasing and then dreaming that it was me in

that hospital bed instead of Alex. I thought, what would Alex have done if I were in her situation? Then I kept thinking that it was my fault she was in a coma because I didn't stand on my own two feet. I let her drag me into practically robbing a liquor store, I let her almost get me into a car with her when she was stoned, and I never let anyone know that she needed help. It was really too much for me to handle anymore. So I sat next to her bed and whispered to her to try explain myself.

"Alex, it's me, Deonna. I know you probably can't hear me, but I've got to try and tell you anyway. It's not that I'm not your friend or anything, but I can't keep going along with the program anymore. Maybe you could keep quiet if this were happening to you, but that's because you're different. You're Alex and I'm me. I'm just plain and simple. You need all kinds of things that I can't figure out. And now you're lying there like a vegetable. What good are you that way? You might have turned me into one, too. Well, that's not going to happen to me. I'm going to be great someday. But not if I have to hold this whole thing in for the rest of my life. Dave's life is over your head, but you're practically dead so it doesn't matter to you. Maybe nothing ever did. But now your life is hanging over my head, and it matters a lot, Alex. It really matters. So I'm telling your mom everything. Then maybe I'll tell my parents everything. I'm not sure what good it would do, though. I already know what I did wrong, and I'm not going to let it happen again. Someone's got to show you that they care enough about you that they'd do something for you even if you didn't like it. I wish it wasn't me, but it is me. Whatever happens. . .it'll just have to happen. We were friends because we believed in each other, but I believe in living and you don't. I wish you'd wake up first, but you probably never will."

Then I put my head on the rails of her bed and cried so hard that my stomach hurt. I knew everything was going to

change as soon as I walked out of that room. A cold wind blew into the room right then and made the drapes slap against the wall. I had been watching those horses dance on the drapes for two weeks and they had never jumped around like that. It made me look up. That's when I saw that Alex's eyes were open!

"You're alive! You're not dead! Wow, I can't believe it!" I shook her arm through the railing.

Alex looked at me for a long time. I guess she couldn't talk. Her eyes kept closing like she was falling asleep, but then she'd open them again and just stare.

"You heard me? If you did, squeeze my hand," I said, and put my hand in hers. It wasn't as cold as it usually was. She squeezed my hand just a tiny little bit. So she knew I was going to tell her mom. I pushed the button on the nightstand to get the nurse in there. Alex was moving her lips.

"What? Say anything. Say you hate me, I don't care."

She stared at me for maybe thirty seconds, but it seemed like it was a lot longer. A tube kept her from speaking, but if she really wanted to, Alex could find a way to give me a piece of her mind. Someday, I'll learn how to give her a piece of mine when it will do the most good. See, the greatest thing about Alex is that even though she's pretty tough on the outside, she's really as soft as a pillow on the inside. I'm exactly the same way, and maybe that's why neither of us had to say a word. We both knew that everything would be okay.